GW00400091

Housebound Store

War on the Pecos

War on the Pecos

ELLIOT CONWAY

A Black Horse Western

ROBERT HALE · LONDON

© Elliot Conway 2000
First published in Great Britain 2000

ISBN 0 7090 6704 6

Robert Hale Limited
Clerkenwell House
Clerkenwell Green
London EC1R 0HT

Typeset by
Derek Doyle & Associates, Liverpool.
Printed and bound in Great Britain by
WBC Book Manufacturers Limited, Bridgend.

For the pupils and staff of Longfield
for making me feel so welcome

ONE

Texas Ranger Captain Simpson T. Jack held up his hand to bring his eight-man detail to a dust-raising halt. Ahead of him lay the long, dark mass of high, steep buttes, hog-back ridges and blind canyons. There was a way through the rocky tangle, a narrow twisting trail: ideal territory, the captain thought, for the band of Apache broncos they were tracking to draw blood from any pursuer careless enough to get too close to them.

'What do you think, Brad?' he said, without taking his calculating gaze from the mountains.

Brad, a wiry, grey-stubble-cheeked Ranger was a born plainsman and hadn't lived so long fighting bad-ass Indians and Mexicans without having strong opinions on possible dangerous situations without having to ponder too long over them. 'The wild boys could be headin' straight through Broken Rock Canyon, Capt'n,' he said. 'On their way to join up with that bloodthirsty

7

sonuvabitch, Geronimo, in his hole-up in the
Sierra Madre, bein' I reckon, that's why they
sneaked off the San Carlos Agency. But the
Apache, as you well know, Capt'n, make up their
plans on the move. If they spot an advantage
comin' their way they'll act upon it, pretty damn
quick.' Brad spat a stream of tobacco juice
between his horse's ears. 'Like them sittin' up the
ridges waitin' for us to show up in front of their
Winchester sights.'

Captain Jack twisted ass in his saddle and
looked at the Ranger alongside Brad. 'Is that the
way you read it, Sam?'

Sam gave the captain a look of surprise. How
else was there to read the situation? It puzzled
him to think that the captain, who had been
killing hostiles of all shades of colour since he was
britched, and known along both sides of the Rio
Grande as one of the top manhunters in Texas,
had to ask such a question.

'Ain't no other way to read it, Capt'n,' he said.
'That's if we want to keep our hair.'

Captain Jack gave a thoughtful grunt. Brad
and Sam were right of course. Riding through
Broken Rock Canyon without first sending rifle-
men in on foot to make sure that likely bush-
whacking spots were clear would be like walking
into Daniel's lion's den blindfolded. But he had
other considerations to take into account. The
band of broncos they were hunting down had,
after they had broken out of the New Mexican

agency, crossed into Texas, killing and burning as they rode south to the border.

If he couldn't capture, or kill them, he had to press them hard, keep them on the move so they would have no time to lift any more Texas scalps, if they wanted to reach Geronimo alive.

'Between the other side of those mountains and the Rio Grande, boys,' he said, 'there's the Barton and Sutton homesteads, women and kids. Think of what savagery those red heathens could inflict on those families if, while we're pussy-footin' through the canyon, they're long gone. They'll know the Rangers and the blue-coats will be hot on their trail and bein' only six of 'em they'll not be lookin' for an all-out fight. Opportunity killin' and burnin' as they're passin' through is more in their way of thinkin'. So I opine, bein' Apache, there'll be a couple of them left behind to act as hold-back boys to win them all the time they can get.' The captain thin-smiled at Brad and Sam. 'If we go fire-ballin' through we'll get past them before they pull off a coupla shots from the single-load rifles they'll be holdin'.'

Sam and Brad favoured him with stone-faced looks, believing he had got it all wrong. He wasn't so sure either, but he had to take that risk. Though he knew the pair, and the rest of the detail, would follow him to the gates of hell, and through if he gave the order. After all he was their captain. An hour or so later he was to find out just how wrong he had been.

The Apache, the whole band, cut loose at them with repeating rifles, as they slowed their mounts riding across a rock-strewn stretch of the trail. The patrol had entered the canyon at a fast pace, rifles drawn, ready for quick action, eyes scanning high on both sides of the trail. The first sound of the firing had the Rangers lying low on their horses, rib-kicking them, heedless of the danger of them stumbling, galloping over the rough ground.

Captain Jack heard the cries of men as they were cut down by the deadly hail. His horse caught a shell in its right flank that sent it rearing and squealing, almost unseating him, causing him to drop his rifle. Then, maddened with pain, it turned and bolted along a narrow winding cleft in a split-faced butte. No amount of rein jerking and cursing could slow its hoof-spark-raising charge. Part way in, his head struck a jutting out piece of rock and he fell forward across his saddle-horn sick with pain and almost blinded by the blood pouring from the gash on his temple.

The reins hung slack between his fingers and his knees lost their grip on the horse. He let go of the reins, kicked his feet out of the stirrups and slid backwards out of the saddle to avoid having a leg trapped in a stirrup iron and being bounced along the trail getting his head stove in. He landed heavily and awkwardly on the rocky ground, hearing a bone crack in his arm. He experienced a fresh stab of pain, then passed out.

When he came round, the captain had difficulty

in seeing through his blood-caked left eye. Holding his broken arm he struggled painfully to his feet, feeling as though he had been pistol-whipped and most of his bones had been jarred out of their joints. And there was no sign of his horse. He had no idea how long he had been out cold, but it had been too long for him to have been away from his men fighting for their lives. Jaws clamped tight shut to hold in the pain, he set off in a hurried unsteady-legged walk back to the main canyon.

The captain could hear no echoing sounds of gunfire as he made his way along the cleft and opined that the Apache had broken off the fight, won the time they wanted and were now well on their way south and his men could be searching for him. It was a thought he didn't really believe. He was having a strong foreboding that things were going to turn out as black as they could be.

The faint, hoarse-throated cries he heard as he neared the cleft's opening raised the hair at the nape of his neck, made him forget his own aches and pains. His ominous feelings were about to become a blood-chilling reality. He stepped out on the main trail, pistol fisted and cocked, face a death's head mask, not caring a hoot if the Apache were standing there waiting for him and determined to send as many of the sons-of-bitches to Hell before they despatched him to wherever he was bound for in the after-life.

There were no waiting broncos in the canyon,

just the bodies of his men and the bulkier corpses of the slaughtered horses dotted across the ground. The dead Rangers, he could see, had been disembowelled and scalped, their stomach-heaving mutilations black with a covering of angry buzzing flies. They had been the lucky ones, shot dead before the Apache had done their fiendish work on them with their knives.

The pitiful cries he had heard came from Brad and Sam, staked out on the ground. Their cries now only low-pitched, lung-exhausted moans. The bile rushed up into the captain's throat when he saw that their bodies were oozing red messes; they had been skinned alive. He didn't think it possible! that men could stay alive for so long suffering such agony. He also saw the unspoken pleas in the death-dimming eyes for him to put an end to their torment as clear as if Brad and Sam had shouted it out. With tears streaming down his face and a pistol hand that trembled, he squeezed the trigger of the Colt. The sounds of the two merciful shots bounced along the ridges, echoing like the bells of Hell in his ears.

After that everything became a blur to the captain. Sobbing, cursing, hymn-singing, he one-handedly dragged the bodies together and began to cover them with stones to act as a temporary grave.

Two ranch-hands, looking for strays, found him there, still working at his grim task. 'Jeez, Wal,' one of them said, as he took in the captain's bloodied face and hands and dust-shrouded clothes. 'The state he's in he should be lyin' alongside the fellas he's coverin' up.' Both riders dismounted and walked across to the captain.

'Ease up, old-timer,' Wal said, kindly. 'Me and Bobby here will see to the buryin'. You rest up a spell in the shade over there, then you can ride back with us to the big house and get those cuts seen to before they go bad on you.'

Captain Jack glared up at them, mad-eyed. 'This ain't a regular burial!' he almost shouted. 'Now one of you haul ass back to that ranch-house and tell the big man that Captain Jack of the Texas Rangers needs to borrow one of his wagons so he can take his men in for a decent Christian burial at Presido, *comprende*, *amigos*? Get goin' or I'll draw out my pistol and plug you both.'

Wal and Bobby looked at one another, each thinking that the Ranger captain meant what he said about pumping holes in them if they didn't carry out his orders, both knowing men who are loco don't listen to reason.

'I'll bring out the flat-bed, Capt'n,' Wal said. 'Bobby will stay here and get the bodies ready for loadin' on the wagon. 'And as I said, get yourself outa the sun or Bobby will be stackin' you on the wagon for the trip to Presido. I should be back in a coupla hours or so.' Wal lifted his canteen from the saddle-horn and handed it to the captain.

Captain Jack took a mouthful then poured some of the water over his head and sank back to the ground sighing deeply, his face etched with dark lines of pain and exhaustion.

'Boys,' he croaked. 'I'm right sorry I spoke harshly to you, but as you can see it ain't been the best of days for me. Now go and get that wagon and I'll be beholden to you.'

Captain Jack made it back to Presido alive, though he'd aged twenty years. The loss of his men had hit him hard and he no longer felt he had the confidence it took to be a Ranger captain, or the right, so he handed in his badge and took to hitting the bottle to try and blot out the sight of the butchered bodies and cries of the men he had so foolishly led to their deaths.

TWO

Young Floyd Bishop watched with growing disbelief the small-built man making his way to the shack in the swaying, tangle-footed gait of a man well liquored up. Could he really be the fearless Texas Ranger, Captain Jack! he asked himself, one of the greatest manhunters in the Lone Star State? A man whose deadly accuracy with a Winchester rifle and the Colt pistol and doggedness on the trail struck fear into the hearts of outlaws along both sides of the Rio Grande as far west as the Panhandle?

A downcast-faced Floyd gave his kid sister a thin smile. 'He sure don't have the cut of a feared lawman, Belle,' he said. 'But it must be the captain. The smith told us back there in Presido that the captain had quit bein' a Ranger but still lived in the last shack before the ford across the Rio Grande.'

Belle gave her brother a withering look. She

had been against Floyd's idea of spending what little cash they had in the hope of hiring Captain Jack to help them get back their farm.

'Let Uncle Slater have the place,' she had told him. 'I can't see the *famous* Captain Jack riding all the way here from Presido, Texas, to help out two young farmers. He'll probably tell us that it's the New Mexican law authorities' task to sort out our problem. Let's quit the holding and leave for Fort Sumner, I'll find work in one of the stores there. You can hire yourself out as a ranch-hand to Mr Chisum. The Jingle Bob ranch is always looking for men.'

Floyd knew that Belle was talking sense. There was no guarantee that Captain Jack would come to their aid even though their pa had saved the captain's life in Mexico when he had served in the captain's Ranger company. But, damn it, he thought angrily, it was his and Belle's holding, not his uncle's.

Belle saw Floyd's face steel over into unyielding stubborn lines, like their pa's did when he would brook no one telling him otherwise when he had come to some decision or other.

'I ain't about to allow Uncle Slater to use our place as a hole-up for the scum he's in cahoots with. He ain't goin' to take off us what Pa and Ma sweated all those years to build up. We're goin' south to Presido to see Captain Jack. He's beholden to us for what Pa did.' He smiled at Belle. 'What can he do to us? If the captain ain't a man of honour he can only turn us down. He won't shoot us.' His face once more hardened. 'At least you'll be out of reach of that sonuvabitch, Seth Palmer's pawin' hands, Belle.'

Belle shuddered. Palmer was one of the stone-faced men, double-armed West Texans, who regularly visited Uncle Slater. She and Floyd hadn't to guess the unlawful nature of the business they discussed with their uncle. Planning more cattle and horse-stealing raids, she and Floyd reckoned. Seth Palmer was the youngest of the outlaw gang, though every bit as cruel-eyed, and fancied himself as a *pistolero*, swaggering about the holding with two pistols sheathed and belted across his waist.

He couldn't keep his hands off her, touching her breasts, her ass, thrusting his body against her as she was working in the kitchen, laughing at her annoyance. She had put up with his pestering so as not to upset Floyd. Palmer, Belle knew, wouldn't hesitate in gunning down Floyd if he confronted the outlaw on her behalf.

'I'll start packing up some supplies, Floyd,' she had said, reluctantly.

They had picked up Mr Goodnight's well-used cattle trail west of Artesia that led north to Wyoming and south to Texas, and almost two weeks later made it to Presido on the Rio Grande, and Captain Jack's cabin. And what she was seeing of the famous Ranger captain, the long uncomfortable ride south had been for nothing.

'We've worn out our horses,' she said, in a told-you-so-voice, 'to try and hire the town drunk!'

'I can't understand it, Belle,' a perplexed-faced Floyd replied. 'Pa used to tell me Captain Jack was one of the greatest outlaw-takers who had ever ridden along the border lands. How the capt'n, though wounded, rode into a rustlers' camp, firin' his pistols, killin' nine of them, sendin' the remainin' two scatterin' for their horses.'

Belle looked, critical-eyed at the swaying, cursing figure of the captain. 'He's sure changed since Pa rode alongside him. Look! He's fallen flat on his face! We'd better go and pick him up before the *famous gunfighter* does himself an injury.' But Floyd was already running across to the captain.

Captain Jack managed to get on to his knees when he felt hands gripping at his shoulders. His whiskey-fuddled brain hadn't yet completely deadened all his instincts of self-preservation. His right hand flickered down to his right hip for his Colt pistol, or where it would have been in his sober, Ranger days.

'I'll help you to your feet, Capt'n Jack,' Floyd said. 'And get you inside.'

Captain Jack twisted his head round and favoured Floyd with a drunk's out-of-focus look. 'Why you nothin' but a kid,' he mouthed. 'And here's me thinkin' I was bein' set upon by some border bad-ass.' Then his eyes suddenly dulled and rolled upwards and he crumpled face down on to the boards again, out to the wide.

'Give me a hand, Sis!' Floyd called. 'He's passed out!'

The smell of whiskey inside the shack was as overpowering as the raw spirit fumes from a backwoods moonshine-still working at full blast. Belle's face wrinkled with disgust. She was all set to tell Floyd she wasn't about to act as nursemaid to a drunken, smelly old man when she realized how disappointed Floyd must be at seeing the man he had built his hopes on being their saviour, unable to make it to his bed. It would, she opined, be like digging the knife in deeper. Not expressing her angry thoughts, and avoiding the empty liquor bottles strewn across the floor as she stepped into the shack, she helped Floyd carry the captain to his cot.

Floyd was disappointed, he was also angry, angry at himself for thinking up the crazy idea of asking a man he did not know to risk his life clearing a bunch of outlaws off his and Belle's land. And angry at Captain Jack for not being the bold-assed law-enforcer his pa had led him to believe he was. Now he would suffer Belle's I-told-you-so looks on the long ride back to Artesia.

Floyd's lips hardened in anger. At least he would make sure the captain knew they had called on him, and why, and what he thought of him sprawled out in a drunken stupor.

'Find a pail, Belle!' he snapped. 'And fill it full of water from that trough outside.'

'It'll take all day to sober him up,' Belle replied.

'He's not only been drinking in the saloons, look at all the empty bottles on the floor.'

'Don't argue!' Floyd said, anger still in his voice. 'I'll sober up the old goat enough for him to know he's had visitors and what we think of him!'

Floyd poured the full pail of water over Captain Jack's head. The icy-cold douche brought the captain back into the world – spluttering and coughing.

'Wha . . . what the hell's goin' on!' he gasped, glaring up at Floyd. 'You've durn near drowned me!'

Floyd dropped the pail and leaned over and grabbed the old Ranger by his coat collar, yanking him up into a sitting position. 'Captain Jack!' he grated. 'You're a miserable specimen of a man, a disgrace to the Rangers. And to think my pa risked his life to save yours!'

The shock of his unexpected shower had cleared the captain's liquor-fuddled brain somewhat, enabling him to think more lucidly than he had been doing for several weeks. 'Your pa saved my life? he said. 'Who the hell are you then? And what right have you to come into a man's home when he's restin' and throw water over him!'

'My Pa was Jim Bishop,' Floyd replied. 'A Ranger in your company. He once told me he got you out of a bad situation one time across in old Mexico. He used to speak highly of you. Though I reckon he would turn over in his grave if he could see you now. I had the foolish notion that you

would help me and my sister to get back our land;
I was willin' to pay for your services.' Floyd
pushed the captain back down on his bed with a
grimace of disgust, 'You'd be as much help as a
drunken agency Injun.' He took hold of Belle's
arm. 'Come on, Sis, we'll ride back home as soon
as we get some supplies for the journey. If we stay
in Presido we might stumble over the famous
Ranger captain lyin' drunk on the boardwalk.'

Captain Jack lay, unmoving, on his cot, wet and
cold, feeling the look the girl cast at him over her
shoulder as she left the shack as painful as a
bullet wound. Being insulted by the kids of the
man who had saved his life sobered him up still
further. Corporal Bishop had been one of the best
Rangers he had ever commanded. Four years ago
he had led a Ranger patrol across the Rio Grande
in pursuit of a bunch of Mexican cattle-lifters. The
raiders, not expecting to see *gringo* lawmen in
Coalhaila, were caught unawares in their camp.

All excepting two of the sons-of-bitches who
had been relieving themselves in a clump of brush
near the camp. They cut loose at him, wounding
him in the arm, causing him to drop his rifle. He
had made a frantic grab for his pistol knowing
that he would have only time to put paid to one of
his attackers before the other one pulled off a
killing shot.

He heard two rapid rifle shots behind him and
both *bandidos* spun round and dropped to the
ground to join the rest of their *compadres* on their

way to Hell. He turned and saw Corporal Bishop grinning at him, and touching the brim of his hat in a salute. Captain Jack gave a bitter laugh. It would have been better if the *bandidos* had killed him that day. Eight good men would still be alive if Corporal Bishop's aim hadn't been so true.

He cast a furtive gaze upwards. The Indians believed that the spirits of their dead watched over them. If Corporal Bishop's spirit was eyeing him now he would be thinking it had been a waste of good lead to have saved his life seeing him lying here drunk and smelling like a hog.

Bishop had left the service and moved to New Mexico just after the raid to try and make it as a sodbuster, a much less dangerous calling than a Ranger. He could understand a man with a wife and a young family not wanting to take too many risks with his life. He hadn't known Bishop had died or he would have made the effort to put in an appearance at his funeral as a mark of respect to his family.

Maudlin tears began to roll down the captain's cheeks. He had let down a lot of men but he'd be damned if he would do likewise with Corporal Bishop's kids. He began to heave himself out of his cot, bleary-eyeing the bottle of whiskey on a nearby chair as he sat on the edge of the cot to steady himself. Captain Jack licked his parched lips. The craving to take several thought deadening pulls at it reached right down into the pit of his stomach.

Cursing loudly, he struck out wildly and swept the bottle off the chair, hearing it shatter on the floor. Before the tempting smell of the spilt liquor overcame his new-born resolve to quit drinking, he stumbled out of the shack and on to the porch and slumped against a roof pole, panting and shaking as though he had run fast over a great distance. He gave a ghost of a smile. The Temperance folk called it the 'Demon' drink, and as sure as hell they were right. But he had fought Apache and Comanche, and beaten them, and those red sons-of-bitches were genuine flesh and blood demons from Hades.

Captain Jack looked at his horse, a dun-coloured Morgan. 'Stonewall,' he said, 'you're in better shape than yours truly, and that's a fact. I never thought I'd climb up on your back again. The smith in Presido has sure taken care of you.'

It was a drawn-faced captain, a shadow of his former self, but his urge for hard liquor had subsided to a dull ache inside him. He had spent the last three days camping on the banks of the Rio Grande, bathing in its cold waters after dark, then baking himself in the blazing sun during the day, and drinking coffee as strong as his stomach could take. The treatment was sweating the alcohol out of his system. He knew it could also kill him. What the hell, he had thought, he'd been as good as dead this past six months.

The captain wore a grey canvas coat that

almost scuffed the ground as he walked, and a flat-crowned, broad-brimmed plains hat. His .44 Dragoon Colt pistol was stuck in the waistband of his pants, for quicker yanking out than any sheathed weapon. He carried another pistol, a .38 Navy Colt, in one of the big patch pockets of his long coat. A Henry 16-load carbine rested in the saddle boot.

He was as ready as he could be, if he didn't crack up on the trail, to meet the trouble the boy spoke of at his place in Artesia, way up there on the Pecos.

THREE

Floyd didn't like the looks the four hard-faced men cast at Belle as they rode slowly past their camp. Belle was kneeling at the fire facing away from them, her hat dangling by its strap on her back, allowing her long blonde hair to fall over her face and neck. Floyd cursed under his breath. He had told his sister to always keep her hat on during the day. At a distance, dressed in baggy pants and a loose-fitting jacket she could pass for his brother.

Pistoleros, *gringo* and Mexican, were regular travellers along the Goodnight trail, men who were always on the look-out for easy pickings. Stealing two horses and their gear and whatever else was in their camp that took their fancy, wouldn't raise any sweat, or cause consciences to prick in suchlike taking men. And the added bonus of a pretty girl to fool around with would make them all that keener to come in with pistols drawn to take what they wanted.

Floyd could see that the four men liked what they were eyeing and once they had downed a few rotgut whiskies at the sutler's store he knew with dreaded certainty they would be paying him a call. Floyd's blood chilled. It would be trouble his pa's old cap and ball Walker Colt, and Belle's rifle, wouldn't be able to hold off. He cursed Captain Jack for landing him in this desperate situation. If he had been sober they would have the added protection of his guns.

Floyd's hopes of a fast, safe ride home, only making camp at night, and then well clear of the trail, were dashed after only a half-a-day's ride in New Mexico. They had caught up with the drag of a large herd pushing north. The slow-moving longhorns were spread out on both sides of the trail, forcing them to cut across a stretch of broken ground to get ahead of the herd.

The horses were picking their nervous-footed way down a loose-banked dry wash when Belle's mount stumbled, almost unseating her, and slid the rest of the way down a moving bed of shale on its haunches, raising dust clouds. Once on the floor of the wash, Belle quickly dismounted and while calming the animal checked it over to see if it had suffered any injury.

'Damn it, Floyd!' she said. 'She's holding up her right leg! It don't feel as though there's any bones broken so I guess it's only sprained!'

That meant they had to make camp here for several days until the horse could put its foot back

on the ground again. The nearest water for their
use and to wet bandages for the horse to bring the
swelling down, was the creek they had crossed
this side of the sutler's store.

Floyd watched the riders dismount at the store
and give the camp another long look before they
went inside. He prayed real hard for them to
continue to ride south when they'd had their fill of
whiskey, a prayer he hadn't much faith in. Not
telling Belle his fears, he walked as casually as he
could to his gear and drew the Walker out of its
sheath, checked its loads then stuffed it inside his
shirt. He drank his coffee, close-eyeing the store,
his stomach a tight ball of pain.

Captain Jack, coming down from the high ground,
saw the adobe/timber-built building set back a
piece from the the broad, well-trodden cattle trail.
Beyond the shack, he glimpsed the twisting sun-
glinting sheen of a creek. A good place, he
thought, to feed and water Stonewall, and to ease
his aching back and ass. It was as though he had
never sat up on a horse in his life.

He still felt as if he was just pulling through
after a bad attack of swamp fever, but his craving
for the demon drink was now only a dying flicker
in his brain. He had managed to partake of some
food earlier on in the day, and kept it in his stomach. He wasn't steady-handed enough yet to put
an open razor to his face, but he had clipped his
beard to an inch or two from his chin and opined

he no longer had the look of a washed-out Old Testament prophet.

He drew up his horse outside what he could see now was a sutler's store noting the broken crates and feed sacks stacked on the porch, and the four horses tethered outside. It would give him the opportunity to buy some extra feed for Stonewall before riding on to the water.

As he dismounted, he could see that the horses had been ill-used. His face hardened. Men who badly treated their horses wouldn't be *hombres* flowing with the milk of human kindness. Taking an old man's horse and gear would come as natural to them as breathing. He pulled the Henry out of its boot and levered a shell into the chamber. Next he drew back the skirts of his coat so that the butt of the Dragoon could be clearly seen. Not preparing for the worst in any given situation could get men killed, as he so bitterly knew.

He pushed open the splayed, jointed door and walked inside in a real stomping-man's stride and bellied up to the two planks resting on barrel heads that did service as the store's bar counter. He laid down his rifle, heavily on the planks, half turning so that he could access the four men who were sitting drinking at the only table in the store.

When his eyes had adjusted to the dimness of the place, he knew his judgement of them had been right. The four had the mean-eyed, pinched-

faced looks of men who had never pocketed an
honest earned dollar in their adult lives. He
favoured them with a stone-faced look, letting
them know that tangling with him would mean
big trouble for them.

The sutler, a heavy-jowelled, big-bellied man,
thought his new customer, wearing an old coat
long enough to trip him up, was an old saddle
bum and was about to ask him to show him the
colour of his money before he put the whiskey
bottle on the bar. When the old man turned face
on to him he knew just how wrong he had been.
Killers, hard men of all shades of colours and
ages, had called in at his store. The four sitting at
the table had flyers posted on them for shootings
and knifings, but their faces were angelic
compared to the old man's. Gazing at it was as
blood-freezing as having a knife blade at his
throat.

The sutler tried hard to make his welcoming
smile the real thing. 'Whisky, *amigo*?' he said. 'I've
some special in the back, genuine Scotch.'

As genuine as your smile, you oily-faced son-of-
a-bitch, the captain thought. 'No thanks, friend,'
he replied. 'Though I'd appreciate some coffee.
Then I'll buy some feed for my horse.'

'Coffee?' The sutler gave the captain a narrow-
eyed look of surprise. If the old goat hadn't had
the cut of a desperado about him he would have
told him that he wasn't running some fancy tea-
and coffee-drinking place. Instead he said, 'Yeah,

sure, coffee it is. I'll just go into the kitchen and boil up some water.'

'You do just that, pilgrim,' replied the captain. 'I ain't in a pressin' hurry.' In fact he didn't want any coffee; he had drunk enough of the stuff to have filled a fair-sized barrel. He wanted the four hardcases to ride out before continuing his journey. Four men back-trailing him with evil intentions towards him in their hearts wasn't a hazard he wanted to take on. The captain smiled inwardly. Though if the sons-of-bitches didn't pull out soon he would help them to think that they had overstayed their welcome here by putting a few Henry slugs about their ears.

He was drinking his coffee when he heard one of the four laugh loudly and say, 'OK, boys, let's go down to the creek and have some fun before we hit the trail.'

It was the big man with the knife-scarred face who had spoken and the captain opined that it wouldn't be a laughing matter for whoever it was at the creek they intended having fun with. But at least they were going to move on, south he hoped.

The captain was on the store porch filling a gunny sack with feed when he heard the screams. He didn't know why he should have known it was Corporal Bishop's daughter who was doing the screaming. She had only spoken a few words in his presence and he had been drunk at the time. He had thought she and her brother would have almost made it home by now. He put it down to

the fact that females travelling along Charlie
Goodnight's cattle trail were few and far between.

He gimlet-eyed the sutler standing in the doorway. 'As you heard,' he said, 'there appears to be
trouble goin' on down at the creek. And I'm reckonin' on takin' part in it. I'm trustin' that you've
got the savvy not to take sides agin me, or I'll ride
back here and burn this rat hole down about your
ears – then I'll shoot them off. *Comprende, amigo?*'

The sutler had to swallow hard before he could
trust himself to answer. 'Mister,' he croaked, 'me
and trouble don't mix, and that's the truth. I'm
goin' inside, barring this door and run a check on
my stock.'

'Good,' replied the captain. 'A man lives longer
if he acts sensible.' He picked up the Henry lean-
ing up against the wall of the store then mounted
Stonewall and rode down to the creek. He could
see the smoke wisp of a campfire on the far side of
the creek, the camp hidden by a thick belt of
brush, and cut away to his right to cross the creek
further upstream, acting as sensibly as the sutler
was doing. He had tried going blindfold into a
hairy situation before and it had ended in one big
bloody mess. The four roughnecks wouldn't expect
trouble to come at them from behind, or so he was
figuring.

Floyd was squatting at the edge of the creek
cleaning the pans and plates. He had been
tempted to break camp and take a chance that
Belle's horse could be ridden. Then again, he had

thought, he was risking crippling the horse
permanently, a long ways from home for nothing.
The men he was worrying about could continue
their ride south once they had finished their
drinking session.

Suddenly, behind him, he heard the ominous
click of a pistol being cocked and he realized fearfully he'd had every reason to have been worried.

'You just get to your feet, arms held high, boy,'
he heard a voice say. 'And there'll be no need for
me to plug you.'

Arms grabbing air, silently cursing a blue
streak for allowing himself to be caught off guard,
Floyd stood up slowly, and turned and faced the
man, and the ominous black muzzle-hole of the
gun aimed at his head, by the man who had
sneaked up on him. Suddenly he heard Belle
scream and, heedless of the pointed gun, instantly
made a move to go to her aid. The savage blow on
the side of the head from the gunman's pistol
knocked him to his knees. Pain-dazed, he sensed
his gun being pulled out of the top of his pants
then being hauled, stumble-footed, back to the
camp.

Belle had also been caught unawares. She
hadn't known of her imminent danger until three
men stepped out of the brush in front of her.
Horrified, seeing her fate mirrored in the evil-
smiling faces, she dashed for her rifle lying on the
ground by the fire. She hadn't taken three paces
when one of the man grabbed her by the waist

and clutched her tightly to him. Screaming wildly she kicked and struggled to break his hold on her.

The man grinned at her futile efforts and held her even tighter. 'Now don't go and tire yourself out, missy,' he said. 'You've gotta have the strength to please four of us!'

She thought frantically of what could have happened to Floyd, fearing for his safety. Had he been killed? But she hadn't heard the sounds of gunfire. When she saw him being dragged into the camp she began to shriek words at her attacker she had never thought would have passed her lips, and redoubled her fighting to break free so that she could run to Floyd to see how badly he was injured.

Her cries brought Floyd back to his senses and he saw Belle fighting like a wildcat in the arms of one of the gunmen. 'You dirty sonuvabitch!' he yelled, crazy-eyed. 'Leave my sister be!' he said wriggling and twisting in his captor's hands. And got another pistol whipping. His head seemed to burst with pain and he fell to the ground totally unconscious. Belle's screams reached a higher pitch.

Then Captain Jack came into view. He stood, straddle-legged, rifle held high across his chest for a few seconds, taking in the scene.

'Well lookee here, Luke,' the gunman who had felled Floyd said. 'The old goat's come sniffin' around!'

Luke hugged Belle and grinned at the captain.

'You'll have to wait your turn before you can get your way with this purty little thing, old-timer.' His lecherous grin froze when he noticed the 'old man's' stone-faced expression, then turned into a look of fear and alarm, then into a mask of pain, as he took a Henry shell in his right shoulder. Howling like a kicked dog he fell away from Belle, holding his arm, bent double in agony.

The captain caught sight of one of the other gunmen's hands flickering down to his pistol. The Henry barked and flamed again. The man spun round and found he couldn't keep his balance after a heavy slug had ripped its bloody, agonizing way through his thigh and collapsed to the ground, his moans of pain echoing his *compadre*'s.

Captain Jack fish-eyed the two unwounded men, rifle held steady on them as Belle ran across to her brother.

'There's another fourteen loads left in this long gun, *amigos*,' he said. 'Make a foolish move, like those buddies of yours rollin' about on the ground there, and you'll get your share. You're lucky I ain't in a killin' mood or I wouldn't be talkin' to you, I'd be raisin' a sweat plantin' y'all. Now shed your gunbelts and throw them my way, then get to your pards and do likewise.' While watching the gunmen doing as they had been ordered, he shouted over his shoulder at Belle, asking if her brother was OK.

Both unwounded gunmen glanced nervously at each other, both gabbling silent prayers that the kid was OK or the old bastard would have them down on the ground groaning and sobbing like Luke and Cliff.

'Yes, he's all right, Captain Jack!' a much relieved Belle said. 'He's coming round!'

'You help him down to the crick and bathe that gash,' Captain Jack said. 'My horse is back there in the brush. In one of the saddle-bags there's a jar of ointment. It's a genuine Comanche concoction, stinks like a dead polecat, but it keeps wounds from goin' bad.' He fierce-grinned at the gunmen. 'There ain't anyone here goin' to pester you again, missy, so take your time.' He pointed his rifle at the two men on the ground. 'And those boys need attendin' to before they bleed dry. And while you're aidin' them, still keep thinkin' peaceful thoughts or this camp will be swimmin' in blood.'

FOUR

They were ready to ride north. The unwounded gunmen had been given a final warning by the captain. 'Pilgrims,' he had said, 'if I see as much as your trail dust doggin' our trail I'll come fire-ballin' back and put you down for good.'

Belle was up on the horse of the man who had molested her, the captain telling her the son-of-a-bitch owed her something for what he had put her through.

Two hours' hard riding from the creek, Captain Jack, who was at the rear watching their back trail, felt all in. Only his stubborn pride in the presence of two youngsters kept him sitting in his saddle. So when they reached the foot of a rock ridge, commanding a clear view of the way they had travelled, he called for Floyd and Belle to halt.

'I reckon we should make camp up amongst those rocks,' he said. 'It should make a good look-out spot, even after dark.'

37

Once they had made it up on to the ridge and
were unsaddling the horses, Floyd noticed the
deep lines of exhaustion on the captain's face. He
opined it had been nothing less than a miracle for
the old man to have ridden all the way from
Presido, then get the better of four gunmen when
the last time he had seen him he had been dead
drunk. He cast a significant glance at Belle.

'Me and Belle will fix us some chow, Captain
Jack,' he said. 'And stand the watches. Ain't that
so, Belle?'

'It's the least we can do,' replied Belle, 'for what
you've done for us. You rest up a while, we'll see to
everything.'

Captain Jack gave them a weary-faced grin.
'Well,' he said, 'that's mighty appreciated, bein'
that I ain't so young as used to be, not by a long
chalk; that and the tryin' time I've been through
lately I sure could do with getting stretched out
on my bedroll for a few hours. But if you see or
hear anything that bothers you, you wake me up,
pronto-like, understand? In the morning you can
tell me about this trouble you're havin' on your
land.'

'He's fast asleep, Floyd,' Belle said. She had taken
the captain a mug of coffee but had found him
wrapped up in his blanket, hat pulled over his
eys, gently snoring. 'So I didn't wake him up.'

'You did right, Sis,' replied Floyd, sitting on an
outcrop of rock, the captain's Henry rifle laid

across his knees, watching the trail. He was a much sober-minded Floyd, thinking that his decision to seek the captain's help had almost gone terribly wrong. He smiled up at Belle. 'We'll let him sleep as long as he likes. He must have put himself through hell to have caught up with us.'

Belle shuddered, feeling again the hands of the gunman squeezing her breasts painfully. She had been through her own hell. If Captain Jack didn't do anything more for them he had done enough. She would forever be beholden to him for saving her from being raped.

When the captain finally woke up the sun was well above the eastern horizon, and he was embarrassed at having slept so long. Yet he had slept the sleep of the just, undisturbed for the first time by the accusing nightmares of the past months. He caught the appetizing smell of fresh-brewed coffee and frying bacon and, surprisingly, his stomach felt the need for food. He got to his feet without having to put his arms out to steady himself and walked over to a sheltered fall of rocks to relieve himself before making his way to the campfire.

He saw that Floyd was doing the cooking and guessed that his sister was standing the watch. He gave an appreciative grunt. The girl had true grit. The ordeal she had gone through would have made many a girl too upset to sleep, eat, and shun

company. Corporal Bishop would have been proud
of her.

Floyd greeted the captain with a broad grin.
'I've got some chow ready if you fancy eatin'',
Captain,' he said.

Captain Jack grinned back at him. 'Boy,' he
said, 'I could eat an army mule, iron shoes
included. You shouldn't have let me sleep so long.
I ain't entitled to any special favours. I should
have been called hours ago to stand my watch.'

Floyd shrugged. 'There's nothin' been happenin'
here, Captain, that warranted me disturbin' you,'
he replied. 'If there had been we sure would have
woken you up, damn fast.'

'Yeah, well,' mumbled Captain Jack embarrassed, as he sat down at the fire. He grinned
sheepishly at Floyd. 'Thanks for the considera-
tion. It's kinda refreshing to get a good sleep, I
ain't been gettin' restful nights lately.' He took the
mug of coffee and plate of bacon and beans from
Floyd with hands that had lost their trembling,
which brought another satisfied grunt from him.
'Your sister must have a lot of your pa in her,' he
said. 'Like I opine you must have, willin' to fight
for what you think is rightly yours. Now, while I
eat, you tell me about this trouble up there in
Artesia.'

'It's like this, Captain Jack,' Floyd began. 'With
Pa and Ma both dead me and Belle thought the
holdin' belonged to us. Then pa's brother, Uncle
Slater, showed up sayin' that bein' he loaned Pa

some of the money for him to buy the place, he owns half of it. Me and Belle ain't got the money to hire some fancy lawyer to prove whether or not he's entitled to the claim so we couldn't stop him movin' in on us.'

Captain Jack gave Floyd a surprised look. 'You're askin' the wrong *hombre* for help, Floyd,' he said. 'It sounds like lawyers' business gettin' your uncle off your land, even if the money grab-bin' leeches don't come cheap. And that ain't my trade at all.'

'There's more to it than that, Capt'n,' Floyd said. 'Uncle Slater wants to force us out because the holdin' is used by Jake Ketch and his gang of West Texans, five of 'em, as a hole-up. They're a bunch of rustlers. Seth Palmer, one of the gang who fancies himself as a *pistolero*, keeps pesterin' Belle. She puts up with him pawin' at her because she doesn't want me to go up against Palmer.' Floyd looked the captain directly in the eyes. Firm-faced he said, 'But one day I'll have to, Captain Jack, she's my sister and I have to look out for her. Belle says that we should move out before that day comes and I lose out in a pistol fight.'

The captain's lips tightened in hard grim lines. Floyd did need his kind of help. He had to take over as guardian of Corporal Bishop's kids. And he promised himself, whether or not he got them back full ownership of their land, he would make sure that the asshole who fancied himself as a shootist would never force his unwelcome attentions on the girl again, even if that meant calling him out. Providing the Panhandle wild boys didn't plug him, seeing Uncle Slater off the kids' property shouldn't be a big chore. If he could link him in with the rustlers, John Chisum, or whoever's cattle they were lifting, would make sure that Uncle Slater would only have the piece of land he was planted in after his hanging.

'West Texicans, eh, Floyd,' he said. 'Cattle-liftin' comes natural to those boys. The Good Book says that God made man in his own image but that don't apply to them. They're *hombres* who have no relation to the human species. The only law they subscribe to is what Colonel Colt's pistols and Winchester rifles dispense.' The captain favoured Floyd with a direct stare of his own. 'It could be that we may be forced to dish out some of that kind of law ourselves for things to come right for us, Floyd.'

The captain's grin as he finished speaking made Floyd shiver although he was sitting close to the fire. 'I'll take that chance, Capt'n,' he said, bolder than he was feeling.

They both glanced up at Belle as she came up to the fire. She favoured Captain Jack with a beaming smile, which strengthened the captain's resolve to protect her from the West Texan *pistolero*.

'I can see trail dust, Captain Jack,' she said. 'Lots of it and slow moving. It must be another herd coming up the trail.'

'Well, I guess it's time we were makin' dust, folks,' Captain Jack replied. 'If we don't want to get tangled up with a bunch of tetchy longhorns and their ornery drovers.' He smiled at the pair. 'I've slept well and eaten well, so I figure I ought not to be a burden to you on the trail. I'll have to think up the best way I can help you kids. If there's a bunch of cattle-lifters residin' at your place it will have to be a sneaky plan.' He smiled. 'Luckily I've picked up a lot of sneaky tips from *hombres* who are the number one in such-like activities, our red brethren, the Comanche and the Apache.'

FIVE

'Where's the kids, Slater?' Jake Ketch asked. 'They'd been gone days before we rode out to bed down the last bunch of cattle and they still ain't about the place.'

Jake Ketch was a tall, thin, cadaverous-faced man whose gaze kept flickering around as if seeking a place to jump to next if things didn't feel right to him. Handling cattle stolen from John Chisum, the biggest rancher in the territory, he had to be prepared to move real fast if things turned sour for him. If any of Chisum's hard-riding crew caught up with him he wouldn't see the inside of a jailhouse, he would end up swinging on a rope under the nearest tree.

'There ain't no need to worry because the kids ain't here, Ketch,' Slater replied. 'They'll be across at Fort Sumner seein' if they can find work there. The girl's been tellin' her brother they should sell their share of the holdin' to me and start a new life at Fort Sumner. I know it's damned awkward having them about the place but they ain't got any proof to put to the law that you and your boys are rustlers, Ketch.'

'It would be a cryin' shame if they do quit the place, Slater,' a wide-grinning Palmer said. 'I've taken a real fancy to that purty little niece of yours.'

Ketch swung round, face contorted with anger. 'You've got your brains in your pants, Palmer!' he snarled. 'The girl ain't showing the same feelin's towards you. Take her agin her will and she'll go bawlin' to the law at Fort Sumner. Then we'll have a marshal's posse beatin' a trail here. Even a horn-dog like you can see what problems that could cause us.' He faced Slater once more, bleak-eyeing him. 'Of course that don't mean we may have to kill the kids if they find out we're rustlin' beef, but it'll be done to save all our necks.'

Slater's stomach heaved. Making easy money acting as a hide-out for a bunch of rustlers suited him fine – no risk at all. Even if Ketch and his boys got caught redhanded, being that no stolen cattle were bedded down on his land, he couldn't be tied in with any cattle-lifting. Not so if the kids were killed. That fearful act would need a whole heap of lying to the law to keep him in the clear. Lying, he knew, he couldn't sustain. The rope would be round his neck as well. Slater felt a tightness in his chest, causing him difficulty in breathing.

Ketch saw Slater's unease written on his face.

His smile became icier. 'Runnin' outside the law ain't always an easy ride, Slater,' he said. 'Rustlin' ain't like sodbusting. Me and the boys are all ridin' with a hangman's noose swingin' close by us.'

That didn't cause Slater's stomach to stop its churning. Right now he didn't give a damn whether Ketch and his gang got shot, hanged or roasted alive by wild Indians; he was only worried about his own hide. Ketch's look was also telling him that he would go the same way as the kids if he became a threat to the gang. His choosing of the day when he wanted to quit the rustling business was gone, unless he wanted to quit it dead. The horn-dog Palmer would gun him down with pleasure just to add to his rep. Slater silently cursed his greed, wishing he had never seen the holding, and hoping like hell wherever the kids were, they'd stay there.

'If you follow the Pecos for an hour you'll come to our place, Capt'n,' Floyd said.

The three of them had stopped for a breather on a slight rise overlooking the trail and the river snaking their dual way north. Captain Jack hadn't come up with any plan, grand or otherwise to help Floyd and Belle get full ownership of the farm, other than snooping around to see if any advantage came his way that could nail Uncle Slater as being involved in rustling. Which meant from now on in he had to be working on his own.

He wasn't too keen on Floyd and Belle going back to the farm, but Floyd had insisted, jaw out-thrust at a stubborn angle, just like his pa, the captain thought, he wasn't going to chicken-out in the fight to keep his land.

'I can admire stubbornness in a man, Floyd,' he said serious-faced. 'I'm noted for bein' stubborn myself sometimes, and your pa sure was ornery at times. But don't confuse stubbornness with mule-headness. There's a fine line that separates them and it takes a clear thinkin' man to see it. Could mean the difference between livin' or dyin'. Take for instance this jasper, Palmer. How long can you stand by and let him put his dirty paws on your sister, eh?'

Floyd's face reddened in embarrassment. 'Why, I'd . . . why—"

'Boy!' interrupted the captain, his voice snapping like a whiplash. 'Palmer would gun you down faster than I could spit in your eye and you know it! Then he'd have his way with Belle and your so-called pride would have got you dead, Belle raped, and Uncle Slater crowin' because he's got the whole kit and caboodle. I can see no faster or surer way to lose the farm.' The captain gave a deep sigh of resignation.

'M'be you'll see sense, missy,' he said. 'You know I can't come in with you. If I say I'm an old friend of your father your uncle will naturally opine I'm a Texas Ranger, and if Ketch and his boys are there I can't see them tolerating a Ranger bein' around them, they'll shoot lumps outa me. So I want you to promise that if Palmer gets too much for you to handle you grab your brother by the collar and both of you haul ass off the place, understood?'

A pale, drawn-faced Belle nodded. She looked at her brother and her slight smile brought the colour back into her cheeks again. 'I promise, Captain Jack, she said softly but firmly. 'Even if I have to rope him to his horse.'

'Good,' Captain Jack replied. 'Now, Floyd, give me a layout of the territory hereabouts.'

'As I said, Capt'n,' Floyd said. 'follow the Pecos a piece and you'll come to our place. A half-hour's ride from the holding will bring you to Artesia. It ain't much of a place: a general store, a bar of sorts and a smithy. Ain't but a dozen or so folk there.'

Captain Jack gave a disgruntled snort. Artesia wasn't exactly a rip-roaring, wide-open burg. He couldn't go sneaking around a few shacks unobserved asking his nosy questions.

'Forty miles further west is Fort Sumner,' Floyd continued. 'The law's there, Capt'n. So is Mr Chisum's ranch, he bosses over the biggest spread in New Mexica. His cows bear the Jingle Bob brand on their hides.'

Captain Jack smiled. 'John Chisum and his cattle empire ain't unheard of in Texas, Floyd. Neither is the tall man, Pat Garrett, who upholds the law hereabouts. Though by what I've heard he ain't very successful at doin' it. It seems that William Bonney, alias Billy the Kid, and his young hellions are killin' and liftin' cattle whenever they get the urge. John Chisum, I reckon, will be more than a mite upset at losin' his stock to Billy and will have given orders to his crew to shoot anyone near his cows who they can't vouch for. So that means if I'm goin' to snoop around up here I'll have to keep my head down if I don't want to be tallied as another casualty in the Lincoln County war.'

Captain Jack pulled his horse's head round. 'Now I think it's wise for me to be ridin' on my own. But I'll be keepin' an eye on your place, sneaky-like. So don't think I've quit on you if you don't see me around.' He looked at Floyd for several seconds before he spoke again. 'Remember what I told you, boy, no mule-headed heroics.'

'There won't be, Capt'n,' replied Floyd. 'If there's trouble with Palmer, me and Belle will leave the holdin' and ride for Fort Sumner. So you know where to find us if you don't see us at the farm.'

The pair of them watched the captain until he was swallowed up by the shimmering heat-haze. 'Belle,' Floyd said. 'Let's go home. I've a feeling that everything is goin' to turn out real fine for us. It wasn't a waste of time us makin' the trip to Presido.'

Belle just smiled at him as she kneed her horse into a canter. In spite of having to see Palmer again she was having good feelings about their future. Captain Jack was a man who seemed to inspire confidence in folk.

SIX

Artesia was just as Floyd had described it, the captain thought. Several sun-bleached, splay-planked timbered shacks perched on the west bank of the Pecos. The trail to Fort Sumner, where he was making for, cut away to the left beyond the buildings. He was going to pay a call on John Chisum of the Jingle Bob spread in an attempt to part cover his ass.

He would be moving around territory full of hair-triggered *hombres* and he reckoned that being a stranger in Lincoln County, either of the warring factions could opine he was with the opposition and shoot at him. Chisum's crew would definitely shoot him on sight if he wandered on Jingle Bob land, and he didn't know the boundaries of the Chisum ranch, half of New Mexico by all accounts.

The captain thought that if he could get to see Chisum and explain to him his reason for being in Lincoln County the rancher would oblige him by telling his crew that an old fart, wearing a tent of a coat, had to be left alone to go about his business. Then all he had to do was to keep out of the way of Billy the Kid – and his wild-shooting boys – then he could put his mind to clearing the rustlers off Floyd's land. How he was going to accomplish that he hadn't yet figured out. The captain consoled himself that it was early days yet. He would think of something, his brain was working again: a week ago his brain took all its time to tell him he had to go to the crapper.

He glanced casually at the three men standing on the stoop of the shack still showing a paint-blistered shingle that read, 'Saloon', and favoured them with an old man's empty-faced smile.

The youngest, a mere boy, wearing baggy pants and jacket and a hat more battered than his, and a pistol that weighed heavy at his waist, gave him a buck-toothed grin back. The thin, grave-digger-visaged man's look set the captain's lawman's instincts twitching. It was the mean-eyed suspicious look of a man running one jump ahead of a marshal's posse, quickly assaying him, and just as speedily dismissing him as a threat to his wellbeing. The third man, the captain noted, wore two bone-handled pistols, their sheaths tied down on his legs. He managed a lip-curling sneer and the call of, 'Can't you get a bigger coat than that, old man?' as he passed them. Then he heard the fancy pistolman laugh at his own joke, only faintly though. He was doing some assessing of his own on what he had just seen.

While the captain had to admit there must be scores of West Texas hard men in this corner of New Mexico he had no doubts in his mind that he had been given the once over by the kids' Uncle Slater's cattle-lifting buddy, Mr Ketch. The two-gun man could only be Palmer, Belle's molester, and the youngster with the choirboy's smile must be the much-wanted-by-the-law, Billy the Kid.

The captain smiled to himself. Things were beginning to swing his way. He had proved for certain that Floyd's uncle was in league with a bunch of rustlers; Ketch wouldn't be discussing the price of corn with the Kid. If it came to it he could shoot Slater with a clear conscience, the law being on his side. Ketch hadn't thought him worth a second look. He hoped the next time the shut-faced Ketch looked his way he would have the Henry pointed right at him. Even Billy the Kid had gazed on him kindly though the captain guessed that the Kid would still be smiling fit to bust when he was shooting someone. He had promised himself that he wasn't about to take sides in the county's war, though helping Floyd and his sister meant that he could be interfering in Billy the Kid's rustling business as Ketch must be getting the stolen cows from him. And Billy, by what he had heard, was a tetchy kid to upset. What the hell, the captain thought, if he was fretting about getting shot by a baby-faced kid he should have stayed hitting the bottle back there in Presido.

*

Captain Jack had ridden over a half a mile along the broad wagon trail since passing under the massive wrought-iron gates that signified he was riding across the Jingle Bob's home range, and still he had no sighting of Chisum's big house. He guessed it would be beyond the stand of timber up ahead of him. The range was dotted with bunches of longhorns and he caught the acrid smell of singed hides. Chisum must be branding his mavericks in preparation for drive, he thought.

Two men, up on horses, pulled away from one of the small branding-iron fires and cut across to block his path. The leading rider, a sharp-faced, stocky-built man had the all-seeing-eyed look of a man used to giving out orders. He would be, Captain Jack opined, Chisum's straw boss. The other was an elderly *vaquero*. He pulled up Stonewall and waited for the pair to reach him. It didn't seem as though he was going to be welcomed with open arms for riding across Jingle Bob land uninvited. And he was proved right.

The thickset rider drew up his horse broadside on to Captain Jack's, his hand resting in an intimidatory gesture on the butt of the pistol sheathed on his right hip.

Scowling-faced, he barked, 'You're trespassing on Jingle Bob land, old man. You're lucky you made it this far still breathin'. There's a war goin' on in the territory and we ain't takin' any chances

allowin' strangers to ride free and easy across Mr
Chisum's home range. So turn your horse around
and ride back the way you came while you still
can. The boys will think I'm goin' soft for not plug-
gin' you here and now. Juan, you hurry the old
fart along.'

Captain Jack got a closer look at the *vaquero* as
he nudged his mount nearer, then broke into a
smile. 'That will make a change, Juan,' he said.
'The last time I saw you, leastways your horse's
ass, I was chasin' you and your two brothers back
across the Rio Grande after y'all shot up the best
whorehouse in Presido over some disagreement or
other with the madam runnin' the house.'

Juan's lower jaw dropped in surprise, then
recognition lit up his eyes. '*Madre de Dios!*' he
gasped and, face beaming, he said, 'Thees is no
rustler, Meester Brady, thees is Captain Jack of
the Texas Rangers.'

Brady sat upright in his saddle, his scowl
changing into a look of disbelief. 'The Captain
Jack who gunned down eleven cattle-lifting
sonsuvbitches?'

Captain Jack smiled modestly. 'To keep the
record straight, Mr Brady, I only put paid to nine
of them. The other two fellas hightailed it while I
was reloadin' my Colts. But that was a long time
ago. I reckon I ain't as fast with a pistol nowadays. And ain't as foolish to go up against eleven
men on my own again.'

'What the hell are you doin' so far away from

your bailiwick, Capt'n?' Brady asked, his hard face softening in a smile. 'You ain't thinkin' of nursin' cows?'

'No I ain't!' replied the captain. 'Those four-legged critters are too ornery for me to handle. I've come hopin' to have a talk with the man in the big house, if he's at home.'

'Mr Chisum's up there,' Brady said, pointing at the stand of timber. 'Though I reckon you should meet up with the boss before you get there. He's due to make his rounds any time now. Mr Chisum ain't a sittin'-behind-the-desk boss. You take the Captain up there, Juan. I'll ride out to the south range to warn the boys there that Billy the Kid and his gang have been seen the other side of Fort Sumner. The young sonuvabitch could swing this way and try and lift some of our cows. It's been a pleasure makin' your acquaintance, Capt'n.' He touched the brim of his hat in a salute then rode away.

Captain Jack could have told Brady that Billy was much closer to the Jingle Bob range than Fort Sumner, but he kept that information to himself. When the action started he wanted it to move at his pace, that's if he did manage to get things moving. He grinned at Juan. 'OK, *amigo*, let's go and see the boss man.'

Brady was proved right, before they reached the house a rider came through the timber, dressed in a dark-coloured store suit but wearing a wide-brimmed plains hat.

'That's the *patron*, Señor Chisum, *Capitan*,' Juan said. 'I'll leave you to talk to him, I have to get back and see to the branding.'

'Thanks for speakin' up for me, Juan,' the captain said, and waited for Chisum to come up to him, trusting that he would be as co-operative as his straw boss.

Chisum was smiling broadly when he drew up alongside the captain. 'Howdy Captain,' he said. 'At first I'd thought you had come seeking to be hired and I was all set to tell you that my straw boss does the hiring and the firing on the Jingle Bob spread. I was going to chew his balls off for allowing a saddle-tramp to come up to the big house when I recognized the coat. I opine you could travel the length of the Pecos and the Rio Grande and not see another such-like garb.' He narrow-eyed Captain Jack. 'I heard you quit the Rangers, Captain?' He had also heard the captain was a whiskey soak. But in Chisum's book what a man does in his own time is his own business, unless he chose to talk about it. But he couldn't resist asking the captain if he was OK.

'Yeah, I'm OK, Mr Chisum,' Captain Jack replied. 'The bad times are over.' Then he began to relate to Chisum why he had showed up on his ranch.

The rancher gave him another one of his penetrating looks. 'Not wishing to belittle you in any way, Captain Jack,' he said, 'but it would be a lot healthier for you if you had some of my boys helping you tackle these West Texan scum.'

'That it would, Mr Chisum,' agreed the captain. 'Though that could mean there'd be a lot of wild shells flyin' around and the two kids could get hurt in the crossfire. And if Ketch sees your boys come ridin' in he'll think the kids have sicced them on him and he's mean enough to shoot them. All I would like you to do is to tell your boys if they see me scoutin' around not to plug me for a rustler.' He grinned at the rancher. 'But if things get outa hand I'll sure holler for help.'

Chisum's face twitched in a slight smile. 'I'll pass the word round to my crew that the old *hombre* underneath the big coat hasn't to be shot. Now I've yapped enough. It's time I was checking on how the branding's progressing. I'm trailing a herd north, Wyoming ways, in a few days' time but there'll still be enough men left here on the home range to ride with you if things get out of hand dealing with the West Texans. Good luck in your hunting. It will please me no end to hear that some rustlers have been shot or strung up.'

The captain rode back along the trail with the rancher until they had reached the first of the branding fires. Then after exchanging final farewells, he jabbed his heels in Stonewall's ribs, heading for a look at Floyd's farm and at the comings and goings of his uncle's outlaw friends.

SEVEN

On the ride to the holding, Captain Jack gave the problem of returning the full ownership of the property to Floyd and Belle a great deal of thought. He would have words with Slater, persuade him that it was in his best interests to seek a livelihood well away from Lincoln County. Either he would do just that or Mr Chisum would hear of his involvement in the rustling of Jingle Bob cattle, and him being a lawman the rope was as good as around his neck. Unless Slater felt that he had to commit suicide he would get the hell off the holding.

That still left Ketch and his gang at the farm. They wouldn't be scared off easily. Ketch had a good thing going here. Like driving cattle Billy the Kid had stolen from John Chisum across into the Panhandle for a quick no-questions-asked sale. The holding was a good place to hole-up between raids, much safer for the cattle-lifters than making camp on the open plains, risking the possibility of being visited by Jingle Bob riders who would naturally ask them their business, with cocked rifles in their hands, using them if the answers they got didn't suit them.

It could mean, the captain thought, that he would have to ride in on Ketch and his boys with pistols blazing as he had done with the the the bunch of rustlers he had caught unawares along the Rio Grande. He smiled. Maybe he wasn't as fast with his guns nowadays but he had only half the number of men to shoot down. Though he hoped it wouldn't come to that sort of a showdown. It was no good trying to figure out any plans too far ahead, the captain thought, he would just have to play out events as they came, hoping the breaks came his way.

His first break came sooner than he expected. Out of the coner of his eye he caught a split-second flash of light from a ridge on a line of buttes the trail had been paralleling the last two or three miles. It could have been the the sun's rays reflecting off a rifle barrel, or what he really believed it was, a spy-glass. Whatever it was it meant that someone up there had him under observation. And he would bet his last dollar that someone was one of Ketch's gang standing watch over a bunch-of stolen cattle.

Why else would a man be squatting on a cold, windy ridge unless he was acting as a lookout? Further proof that there was cattle close by was him seeing Ketch and Billy the Kid in Artesia.

Ketch, he reckoned must have been paying the Kid his due for the latest bunch of cattle he had stolen from the Jingle Bob spread.

Captain Jack's plan to clear the rustlers off Floyd's and Belle's land came unexpectedly together by itself. He guessed there would be only a couple of men up there guarding the cattle, The whole gang wouldn't risk coming out into the open until they were ready to move the cattle to Texas. The plan was clear enough. If he could cut Ketch's gang down by two, then scatter the cows, the gang would lose a lot of cash as well as two valuable men. Then, just maybe, Ketch might think it wasn't a paying game to steal cattle in Lincoln County and get to hell back to Texas.

More likely, the captain reasoned, Ketch being a hard man, he would be angry enough to try and hunt down whoever had killed his boys. Here, on the open plains, even if he was past his prime, he would have most of the edge and the advantage of the backing of the Jingle Bob's crew. If Ketch and his boys did come out they would have to keep an eye over their shoulders in case they got jumped by Chisum's men. His plan, the captain concluded, whichever way Ketch reacted to it, would get him and his gang well clear of the holding and the kids.

The captain kept Stonewall moving at a steady pace, looking straight ahead, not wanting to lose his break by alerting the look-out he had been spotted. Further along, he opined, the trail would swing round the end of the range so that there could be the possibility of suprising the rustlers by coming on them by the back door, tomorrow. The light was going too fast now for good clean shooting.

'Who was it, Pike?' Hackett asked in an uptight voice.

Pike lowered his spy-glass and grinned at Hackett. 'Well, it wasn't Pat Garrett, that's for sure. It was some old goat just passin' by. Ain't no need for you to get all upset.'

'I'll be keepin' upset till Ketch gets those cows down there on the trail to the Panhandle,' Hackett grumbled. 'John Chisum and Pat Garrett ain't *hombres* even sharp-thinkin' kids like Bill Bonney can't keep runnin' rings round. One of these days a hanging posse will be tailin' him here. And there's Palmer wantin' us to hang around here awhile because he's sniffin' around Slater's niece. His urges could sicc a whole heap of grief on us.'

'You worry too much,' Pike replied. 'We're earnin' good, easy money, better than we could make in the Panhandle. Across there, the goddamned hired regulators are makin' it too risky to lift even an unbranded maverick. And if Palmer steps outa line Ketch will plug him. Now stop your beefin' and take the glass, it's your watch!'

Still glum-faced Hackett sat down and eyed the trail, thinking that a man couldn't worry enough if taking things easy meant him ending dangling under a hanging tree. He put the glass to his eye and focused it on the lone rider before he was lost from view by a bend in the trail. His morbid mood brightened up somewhat, Pike had been right. The old man wearing a coat that almost covered his horse was only a saddle-bum, no threat to them at all.

EIGHT

Groaning and cursing, Captain Jack swung himself stiffly into his saddle. The long ride from Presido, the six months' heavy drinking and irregular eating habits had taken its toll on him. And a cold night camp hadn't helped any. He was contemplating climbing a hog-back ridge and shooting down at least two owlhoots. The captain gave a tired grin. An *hombre* has to think big once in a while, he thought, or he'd go under.

He was riding west again, on the far side of the high ground, looking for the back door to what would lead him to the valley where he was convinced a bunch of stolen cows were bedded down, banking on the look-out only eyeing the main trail.

Hackett toed Pike awake. 'It's your spell now,' he growled. He shivered and drew his blanket tighter around his shoulders. 'I hope when Cal and Palmer show up they'll tell us that Ketch is goin' to move the herd.'

Pike got to his feet, favouring Hackett with a sour-faced glare. Hackett hadn't the savvy to see that the cows could only be moved when Ketch reckoned it was safe to do so. Hackett's stupid impatience could get them all hanged. He picked up his rifle and with his blanket draped over his shoulders like a serape, made his way to the lookout point.

An aching-limbed Captain Jack paused to allow his lungs to grab several gulps of much needed air. He had hoped he was climbing the right ridge, the twin rocky peaks he had picked out close to where he had seen the sun flashes were silhouetted against the sky way up ahead of him, so it seemed he had guessed right, though the state he was in, a long, long ways ahead, the captain thought dourly.

He had left Stonewall in an opening in the bluff he was scaling, loose and near water. He was risking his life going up against two desperados but there was no reason for Stonewall to put his life on the line. He wasn't the one who was loco. If he didn't make it back down, when Stonewall felt hungry he would go and seek food, and the Morgan had the savvy to know that would be where people were. Some sodbuster, or small rancher, the captain thought, could get himself a windfall of a horse and its gear for free.

He scrambled up a few more yards of shale, finger ends bleeding, knees scraped, wincing as he heard the rattle of a slide of rocks and dirt behind him. He glanced up apprehensively at the rimline expecting to see hard-faced West Texans glaring down at him. If he was forced to fire his rifle, if he had time to unsling it from where he was, hanging only by his toes, the kick would send him ass over elbow back down to the ground, breaking his legs or neck, whatever, as he fell, and an easy target for the rustlers to shoot at. He waited several anxious seconds but saw no sign of movement above him. He began to breathe again and started to climb once more.

The next stretch of the bluff was solid rock and the captain made up some time, then he caught a sound that brought a smile to his sweat and dirt-streaked face: the snorting and snuffling of cattle. He sidled spider-like across the rocks until he could peer over the rim and down into the canyon and see the cows. The captain, begrudgingly, gave Ketch his due as a rustler. It was a dog-legged, blind canyon, the cows bedded down well out of sight of any rider passing the canyon's mouth. Now, he thought came the tricky part.

He had to haul his ass over the ridge, pinpoint where the rustlers were, and gun them down with the Henry before they knew trouble was hitting them. He was trusting he had judged right in thinking there would only be two men guarding the cattle; if there were more they would blow him off the ridge. It needed a diversion of some kind to enable him to get over the rim undetected and the captain opined he had one hell of a diversion at hand. The stampeding cows should provide all the distraction he needed. Close by him there were patches of sun-dried brush and he reached out and pulled up several growths and bundled them into a tumbleweed ball.

Pike, half-turning to shield a lighted match as he lit up his makings, saw a fireball curving downwards into the canyon. 'What the hell!' he gasped, the cigarette dropping from his mouth. Cursing, he snatched for his rifle and leapt to his feet. Pike's second shock was a painful one. The sickening blow on his right shoulder drove him groaning to his knees, and saved his life as Captain Jack's second shot hissed harmlessly over his head.

Pike, sobbing, and dirty-mouthing with pain, ass-slid his way down from the ridge to his horse, in too much of a desperate hurry to escape a killing shot to worry about who was doing the shooting and spooking the cattle, and of the fate of his *compadre* Hackett.

Hackett, sitting half asleep at the fire, had hardly realized that things were going terribly wrong for him and Pike when the captain's third shot caught him full in the chest, sending him flat on to his back, his dying kicks scattering the fire.

Captain Jack, head and shoulders showing above the rim, held his rifle on the spot where the first rustler he had shot had been. He knew he had only winged him, and lucky to have done that being almost too bushed to lift the Henry, let alone hit a target with it. The man at the fire he could see was as dead as any man could be. Satisfied that the man he had wounded hadn't stayed to make a fight of it, the captain heaved himself on to the flat top peak.

He gazed down into the canyon. Through the thick, billowing smoke of the burning grass he heard the frightened bellowing and the thunder of hooves as the longhorns took panic and stampeded out of the canyon. Chisum could be getting back some of his cows he had lost, the captain thought wryly.

When the rustler he had wounded told Ketch of his loss the gang leader would be doing some frantic guessing on just who it was who had caused him this upset, and preparing himself for trouble. Ketch hadn't been pushed into a tight corner yet, and he would want blood or his authority as the boss of the gang would be questioned. Providing he kept himself low, the captain thought, Ketch wouldn't draw his blood and it gave him a fair chance to pick off the gang as they spread out to cut his sign. There could only be five of them, counting the kids' uncle. Though he well knew that he hadn't to get too confident or Stonewall could yet get a new owner. Gingerly he began climbing back down from the ridge to the Morgan.

NINE

It was a disappointed Floyd who walked back to the house from the creek. He had hoped to have seen Captain Jack there. It had been four days since they had parted ways on the trail and while he knew the captain had told him and Belle he wouldn't openly show himself, he had expected, if the captain saw him on his own at the creek, he would have made his presence known. He wondered if the old man had taken to drinking again; after all, he had only quit doing so a few weeks ago and a man of Captain Jack's standing doesn't try and down his thoughts with whiskey unless they were very bad feelings.

The gang had returned to the holding two days ago without Pike and Hackett and he had guessed Ketch had pulled off another cattle raid and Pike and Hackett had been left to guard the cows wherever they had been hidden. Ketch had given him a long, suspicious look, but Floyd hadn't met his gaze in case something showed in his face that

could alert Ketch that his cattle rustling days
could be coning to an end, taking Captain Jack's
warning not to to act foolhardy.

He saw Pike riding in as he neared the house,
face drawn and pale, holding his dark-stained
right hand limply by his side. Floyd grinned and
his gloomy mood vanished. He had no doubts that
Pike had been badly wounded by Captain Jack.
Hackett, it seemed, hadn't been so lucky in his
brush with the old man. He chastized himself for
thinking the captain could be letting him down.

Ketch's angry-looking face as he listened to
what Pike was telling him made Floyd think
Captain Jack must have caused him a lot more
grief than the loss of one of his gang. It didn't take
much figuring out that Ketch had also lost the
stolen cattle. Floyd had often been told by his pa
just how good the captain was at his trade. This
was the second time he had proved that his pa
hadn't been spinning him yarns. Floyd hurried
inside to tell Belle the good news.

'How many of the sonsuvbitches were there?'
Ketch asked, face twisted in mad-eyed rage. Pike
could bleed to death for all he cared. In fact, he
was feeling angry enough to put another shell in
his hide for allowing some bastard to sneak up on
him and spook the cattle.

'I dunno,' replied Pike, rocking on his feet with
pain and loss of blood. 'I only heard one rifle but
that don't mean there could've been more of the
bastards comin' up behind him.'

'What about Hackett?' snapped Ketch. 'Is he followin' you in?'

Pike shook his head. 'The fella who shot me was in a killin' mood. His second shot almost blew my head off. Hackett will still be up there on that ridge, dead, I'd bet on it.'

Ketch gave a non-committal grunt. 'Get inside and have the girl tend to your wound,' he said. He needed time to think. His first thought was that Billy the Kid was behind the shooting. It would appeal to the crazy kid's sense of humour to sell the cows twice over, if the cattle hadn't been stampeded. Likewise, it couldn't have been the Jingle Bob's or Pat Garrett's doing either. The cows wouldn't have been spooked but herded back on to Chisum's land.

A grim smile of understanding crept into Ketch's face, as he came up with the answer to the puzzle. Pike had said whoever it was who had jumped him and Hackett had shot to kill, so spooking the cattle had only been a diversion to enable the shootist to get in close without being spotted. That, Ketch opined, smelled of regulators' tactics.

John Chisum must have hired himself a professional killer, or killers, to protect his cows, though in his experience regulators mostly sneaked about dealing out death on their ownsome. His smile froze into a death's head rictus grin. He would have to do some regulating of his own. He could count on Billy and his boys to back him up.

Billy wouldn't be too happy about the possibility of being framed in the backsights of a regulator's rifle.

Ketch walked into the house to give Slater his orders. He was the only one who could move freely across the territory, being a sodbuster with no links to either faction in the Lincoln County war. He could see to it by contacting Billy's Mexican *amigos* in Fort Sumner that the Kid got the news of how things were turning for the worst for them in the county.

It was a much worried Slater who hit the trail to Fort Sumner to do Ketch's bidding. 'Tell them to let Billy know I want to meet him in Artesia, urgent like,' Ketch had told him. 'Tell them it's regulator trouble; that should get the little killer ass-kickin' it to Artesia.' Regulator trouble – Slater's blood chilled. He cursed the day he had gone into the rustling business with Ketch. Easy money, the mean-faced son-of-a-bitch had said.

Slater gave a brittle, mirthless laugh. More like an easy way of getting himself dead. Regulators were paid bounty money on every rustler they brought in, alive, or more often, as a tarp-wrapped bundle strapped across a horse's ass. And, more disturbing for his peace of mind, they were known to shoot down men whom they just thought could be cattle-lifters. If Ketch and his boys went down, he would fall with them.

Floyd saw his uncle leave with a gut-chewing

look creasing his face. He grinned. What with wounding Pike, the non-appearance of Hackett, Ketch looking as if he could shoot someone, and now his uncle, face twisted as if he wanted to make an urgent trip to the crapper, Captain Jack had sure stirred things up pretty quick for the rustlers.

Then he got to wondering where his uncle was bound for and why. The way Ketch bossed over his uncle it could only be on the rustler's orders he was riding out. It was time he was playing his part in getting his uncle off his property. He wasn't about to let Captain Jack take all the risks. By keeping his ears open he could find out what Ketch's plans were to try and catch Captain Jack, and he could pass the information on to him if and when he showed up at the holding. And he didn't doubt that his sister would be eager to play her part. He was getting the good feeling that it was looking like the beginning of the end for the rustlers on his land.

TEN

Billy the Kid chewed nervously at his lower lip with his buck teeth, his usual wide smile absent from his choirboy face. He had listened silently while Ketch had told him of the loss of the cattle and the strong possibility that Hackett was stoking up the fires of Hell, and how he had reasoned it to be the work of regulators.

He and his boys came and went wherever they pleased in Lincoln County. His Mexican friends informed him of every move Pat Garrett and his deputies made, even how many times the tall man paid a visit to the whorehouse. Regulators were an unknown factor, moving around as unseen as *bronco* Apaches, and every bit as dangerous, striking when least expected, He had heard tales of the sons-of-bitches shooting a suspect rustler while he was pleasuring his wife. He was getting the feeling that he could be hemmed in, something Garrett had never been able to do. On the other hand, there was Chisum's cows crying out to be lifted.

There was only him and Ketch in the bar, the rest of their, respective gangs were out in the street, keen-eyed, rifles held high, taking the regulator threat seriously.

'Regulators, eh,' he said soft-voiced. 'Those *hombres* are bad medicine, Ketch.'

'The worst kind, Billy,' replied Ketch. 'And I don't know how many of the bastards are out there. They could be hunkered down nearby watchin' us right now. You can't lift any of Chisum's longhorns as long as they're roamin' around the county. And sure as hell if you could, me and my boys would be riskin' gettin' plugged drivin' them. If we want to stay in business, Billy, we'll have to try and track them down. Between us we can put ten, eleven men out lookin' for sign. They should be able to cover a lot of likely hole-ups where the regulators could be.'

'Riders scattered all over the place, noses to the ground,' Billy said, 'will alert the regulators we're on to them and they could pull out of the county. Come back later when they think the hunt's died down.' He smiled. 'I've a better idea. I know a Mex, Johnny Bear, who's part Injun. For a coupla bottles of rotgut liquor he'd track a 'roach across White Sands. He's as sneaky as they come. Whoever it is who's causin' us this bother won't suspect a thing till Johnny Bear sticks his knife in his back.'

Ketch managed a smile as he got to his feet. 'Well let's buy us some whiskey then, Billy.

Though tell your 'breed *amigo* to keep the sonuvabitch alive – till we can ask him how many buddies he has with him.'

'Are you ready, Belle?' Floyd asked, face firmer than he was feeling inside. His pa's pistol was stuck in the top of his pants just in case Uncle Slater turned nasty. He noticed Belle's eyes had hard glinting lights in them. She should be carrying the gun, he thought. She had the look of a *pistolero*. He opined she wouldn't hesitate in putting a Colt shell into Slater if he became awkward.

'I'm ready,' Belle replied sharply. 'If we don't make a start to get our *dear* uncle out of our house, poor Captain Jack will be out there till the northers start blowing. And we won't get a better chance, Ketch and the rest of the scum could be back at any time.'

Slater hadn't returned to the holding until early morning so Floyd assumed he had made the round trip to Fort Sumner. What Ketch had sent him there for hadn't taken long but it hadn't made his uncle any happier. Two hours later, he had watched Ketch and his men ride out, including the wounded Pike, along the Artesia trail. Riding with rifles out across saddle-horns, Ketch was going to make a fight of it. And it was time he and Belle began their fight back.

When they strode purposefully inside the house, Floyd noticed Slater was sitting in his pa's favourite chair, which made him angry enough to stiffen his resolve in the showdown with his uncle. He also saw that his kinsman had been hitting the whiskey since he had returned. The almost empty bottle was on the floor by his feet.

Uncle Slater greeted them with a scowl. 'What the hell are you two doin' indoors?' he snarled. 'Ain't the pair of you got chores to do?'

'Yeah, me and Belle have chores to do,' replied Floyd, staring down hard-eyed at his uncle. 'Like makin' you tell us what Ketch and his rustler buddies are up to.'

Slater rocked back in his chair, fear, then anger, flooding into his face. 'Wha— what the hell are you talkin' about?' he blurted out.

Floyd grinned mockingly. 'We know about all the cattle-liftin' that's goin' on,' he said. 'In fact, we know more than you and Ketch about what's goin' on here. We know why Hackett ain't here and who winged Pike.'

Slater gazed, slack-jawed, at Floyd, too dumbfounded to speak.

Seizing his advantage, Floyd pushed the knife in deeper. 'It's friends of ours,' he lied. 'Men who used to ride with Pa, ex-Texas Rangers. Me and Belle didn't go to Fort Sumner last month, we rode south to Presido, Texas to see my pa's old captain, Captain Jack. We told him that you were using our place as a robbers' roost and I wanted you off our land. And now you know they're here.

When they wipe out Ketch and his boys they'll
pay a call here for you. Or tell Mr Chisum's
drovers where there is a man who needs hangin'.
My advice, *Uncle Slater*, is to pack up and move
out. After you tell us where Ketch is now and
what his plans are.'

Slater collapsed like a burst feed sack in his
chair, only fear showing in his features now. He
gazed wildly up at Floyd, hanging on the slender
hope that his nephew was bluffing about Texas
hardmen being in Lincoln County. He could see by
the way the cocky young bastard was grinning his
hope was a forlorn one. He cursed himself for
having such a foolish thought. Who the hell had
shot Pike and spooked the cattle, fairies? Then
with the desperation of a man being pushed to the
brink of a hole on Boot Hill, he found a spark of
whiskey-induced blustering courage.

'They won't rope in Ketch and his gang,' he
sneered. 'He's in Asteria, joinin' up with Billy the
Kid and his boys to hunt down your Texan
friends.' Slater gave a hoarse laugh. 'They'll be
makin' the trip back to Texas in pine boxes. And
you can guess what Palmer will do to you, missy,
when Ketch finds out you've put the Rangers on
him.' The leer he gave Belle made her shiver.

Floyd saw red. 'She's your niece, you dirty
sonuvabitch!' he cried. 'You're supposed to look
out for her!' He yanked out the Walker and
brought it down fast to pistol-whip Slater, cowering in his chair with his hands held protectively

over his head. Belle grabbed his arm in mid-swing.

'Leave him alone, Floyd,' she said cold-voiced. 'He's got no future here and he knows it.'

Floyd, still trembling with rage, reluctantly pushed the pistol back into the waistband of his pants. He gave Slater another fierce-eyed glare and with a curt, 'I'll see you dancin' on the end of a rope, *Uncle*, you can bet on it!' he walked out of the house, pushing Belle in front of him.

On the porch, beyond Slater's hearing, he said, 'Pack some clothes for both of us, Belle. Only the essentials, for the horses will have to carry them. We're leavin'. I'll saddle up the horses.' He glanced back to the open door. 'If it comes to it I'll put a torch to everything that will burn here than let that sonuvabitch in there have it. Go now, and be quick about it.'

Belle could see the sudden change in her brother. He was no longer a youth but a man, as stern-faced determined as their pa had been when facing trouble. She felt proud of him, no longer scared; well not much, she had to admit. She used the back door to go into the house to avoid having to look at her uncle or she might get the urge to throw something at him for ruining their lives.

Floyd had a lot on his mind. He could have Captain Jack's death on his conscience. He was regretting now he had asked for his help. The captain had proved he still had some of his old skill as a manhunter in him and he figured that

he could take on Ketch and his gang, if all the luck
came his way. But luck wasn't going to favour him
for much longer; Billy the Kid and his wild boys
would see to that.

Though the Lincoln County shooting troubles
hadn't reached as far as east on this stretch of the
Pecos, Floyd knew of Billy's rep as a deadly killer.
Captain Jack, even if he hadn't been an old man,
and a newly reformed drunkard, would have no
chance at all facing up to two bands of outlaws.
He would send Belle on her way to Fort Sumner,
which Floyd knew she wouldn't like, then try and
make contact with the captain and explain to him
the new and dangerous situation that had devel-
oped here. Tell him that he had done enough for
the Bishop family; getting himself killed wasn't
part of the deal.

Then he would go back and burn down the only
home he and Belle had ever known, the home in
which his ma and pa had died. It would be a
heart-rending task. Floyd thin-smiled. And just as
heart-rending for Slater watching his investment
burn and his profitable links with Ketch
destroyed. He hurried across to the barn to get
the horses ready.

ELEVEN

Captain Jack sat hunched up over a small smoke-less fire in the shelter of a rocky tumble, praying for the sun to come round to warm his bones after a cold, fitful night's sleep. After his first strike against Ketch and his gang he was having a much needed few hours' rest. Then, knowing trouble was coming his way, he would ride on to the holding to see if he could gather any intelligence there of what Ketch's next moves were by contacting Floyd.

The climbing of the bluff had shown him, if he hadn't already known, how out of condition he was. His recent heavy drinking was something he couldn't easily work off. Maybe resting in a comfortable bed, under a roof, partaking of three squares a day, he could get to feeling as fit as any man on the wrong side of sixty, which was no great shakes considering what he was hoping to achieve. Right now he was living on his nerves and he tried not to think of how much time he had before they cracked.

His tiredness caused him to think that maybe, Ketch, not sure of the odds he was facing, would pull out and go back to Texas. And Ketch might get religion, the captain thought, sourly. His wrong thinking at Broken Rock Canyon and its terrible consequences still weighed heavily on him. Half dead or not, he would have to prepare to do battle with some hard men. If it turned out easier than he had judged he would count that as a bonus.

Floyd and Belle had also spent a cold night. When they had ridden out from the farm and came to the fork in the trail that led to Fort Sumner, Floyd pulled up and told Belle he was staying here to try and contact Captain Jack and tell him about the extra threat he was facing.

'You ride on to Fort Sumner, Belle,' he said. 'I should make it there in a coupla days or so, the Captain's bound to show up soon.'

'I'm staying here with you, Floyd,' Belle said, face set firm. 'And nothing you can say will make me change my mind. From now on, whatever we have to face, we face it together as brother and sister. And as Pa would have wanted us to do.' She narrow-eyed Floyd. 'You don't want me to stay because you intend burning down the house, that's it, isn't it? You think it will upset me.'

'Well it's kinda for that reason, Belle,' Floyd replied, not meeting her accusing gaze. 'It is our home. Ma and Pa died in it, we were born in it! It's like seein' our lives goin' up in smoke.'

'I know,' Belle said, face and voice softer. 'But I'd be a darn sight more upset if we left *Uncle* Slater in it as owner. And remember it was me who first suggested that we should quit the place and make ourselves a new life in Fort Sumner.'

Floyd grinned. 'Oh hell, stay then. You always did get your own durn way. Let's make camp in that brush.' And he swung down from his horse.

Belle sweet-smiled at him. 'I'm entitled to my say, Floyd, half of the holding's mine. You get the fire going, I'll see to the horses.'

Captain Jack decided he had rested enough and was ready as he would ever be to start up the war against Ketch again. Maybe, he thought, he could Indian-up on some of his boys again. He was soon to find out he was the one about to be taken by surprise.

It was Stonewall who gave him the first indication that something wasn't quite as it should be. The Morgan lifted its head high then gave a loud nervous snort. At first the captain thought the animal had caught the smell of a mountain cat, then realized that the wind wasn't blowing from the mountains. Some threat to him was out there closing in.

Acting on the old plains edict of when in doubt prepare for the worst, his hand sneaked towards the Henry lying on the ground near him and he resisted the temptation to look over his shoulder to try and see what had alarmed Stonewall and set the hairs on the back of his neck twitching.

His fingers had just touched the rifle stock when a heavy weight fell on him, pushing his face down between his knees with such force that he gasped in pain. The captain rolled over on to his side, throwing his attacker over his right shoulder. Johnny Bear cursed as the red hot embers singed the fringed ends of his raggedy-assed buckskin pants. Turning swiftly as a cat, he reached out with his fisted pistol and struck the captain on the side of the head with the barrel. The captain groaned, saw a myriad of flashing lights, then everything went black for him.

Johnny Bear got to his feet and kicked his unconscious victim in the ribs just to make certain that he was really knocked out. He gave a grunt of surprise when he saw it was an old man, seemingly twice his age. He had been led to believe that he was tracking down a bunch of regulators. He had cut no other fresh sign hereabouts. Old he may be, he thought, but the son-of-a-bitch had almost drawn his pistol. A couple of seconds the wrong way and the old goat could have been gazing down at him. Of course, he could have finished him off with a rifle shot without coming into the camp, but Billy had told him he wanted whoever he captured brought in to Artesia for questioning.

When Captain Jack came to, he was up on his horse, hands tied to the saddle-horn and with a head that felt it had been kicked by an army mule. They were riding away from the Pecos so he opined he was being taken to Artesia. He shot a sidelong glance at his captor, an expressionless, hatchet-faced 'breed, an *hombre* who, he knew, wouldn't be caught napping by any fancy tricks he might try, if he knew of any.

He must have been living in Dream Land to think he could keep on top of things as he could in the old days. He had sure underestimated Ketch's reaction to the threat he posed against him and he would pay for it with his life. The only reason the 'breed hadn't killed him off was that Ketch would want to question him to find out exactly what he was up against. He should have accepted the fact that he was an old man and ought to be sitting in a rocking-chair on some front stoop not hard-assing it out here and getting cold-cocked by a sneaky son-of-a-bitch pussy-footing up on him.

'Riders comin' our way, Belle,' Floyd called out. 'Two of 'em. They could be Ketch's men goin' back to the holdin'. You'd better take the horses deeper into the brush; we don't want them to spot us.' He began toeing dirt on the fire to extinguish it.

If they were two of Ketch's men and saw them they would wonder why they were camping out here seven, eight miles from the farm. Uncle Slater would put them wise as to why his nephew and niece were here, then, like Captain Jack, they would become the hunted.

'Hold on, Belle,' he said. 'One of them's the

captain, I recognize his coat.' He shot an alarmed look at Belle. 'The captain ain't sittin' right on his horse, I think he's the other fella's prisoner!'

'Then we'll just have to rescue him then, won't we?' replied Belle.

'Yeah, I reckon we oughta,' Floyd said, staring at his sister in amazement. He was seeing her in a new light. Not so long ago he was teasing her, pulling at her pigtails, now she held her peashooter rifle with the determined true grit of a real live plainswoman. He was real proud of her. He gave her a tight-faced grin. 'Let s do it then, Belle,' and he drew out the Walker and thumbed back the hammer. He didn't relate to Belle that though there was only one man to throw down on he had the cut of a bad-assed *pistolero*, the killing breed.

Johnny Bear was thinking of the bottles of whiskey waiting for him in Artesia when he handed over his captive, when suddenly his found himself confronted by two *gringo* kids. The boy was holding in his two hands a long barrelled pistol. The girl held a piddling small bore varmint rifle on him.

'Just pull up your horse, mister, and hand over your prisoner and you won't come to no harm,' Floyd said boldly, thinking he couldn't hit a barn door the way his hands were shaking. The man this close up looked even more frightening. He had never drawn a bead on a man before and fleetingly wondered if he had the nerve to pull the trigger if forced to.

Johnny Bear showed glinting gold teeth in a fearsome smile as his right hand flashed to the pistol sheathed on his hip. A jumpy-nerved Floyd jerked the trigger of the Walker to only hear a dull ominous click. Shit! his brain screamed, a misfire, Belle's wild shot only whizzed skywards yards way from the *pistolero*. In a panic, Floyd yanked the trigger back for another shot though clearly knowing he would be dead before he fired it, seeing the *pistolero*'s gun swinging down on him.

The sharp crack of a rifle from behind him made Floyd jump and Johnny Bear's smile was lost forever under a fearful mask of blood and shattered bone as the Winchester shell tore through his head. The 'breed snapped back in his saddle, the unfired pistol dropping from his hand. He slipped sideways out of his saddle to hit the ground with a dirt-raising thud. His horse, smelling blood, stepped skitterishly away from its now dead owner.

Floyd swung round to see who had performed the life-saving miracle. He saw a tall, heavily moustached man dressed in a faded duster and holding a rifle high up across his chest, step out of the brush. Floyd, still in shock, gave him a weak but heartfelt smile of thanks.

'That sonuvabitch was all set to down me.' He looked at an equally ashen-faced Belle. 'And my sister, if you hadn't showed up when you did, Mr Garrett.'

'That he would, boy, that he would, with great pleasure,' Marshal Garrett replied. 'Taking on a no-good *hombre* like Johnny Bear was a foolhardy thing to do. There's four outstanding warrants out on that 'breed for murder and horse-stealing. Another two would have boosted up his rep somewhat. I take it the old man is an *amigo* of yours?'

'Old man!' Floyd had lost enough of his fear to sound indignant. 'Why that's Captain Jack, the Texas Ranger! He's come all the way from Presido to help out me and my sister, Mr Garrett!'

Marshal Pat Garrett took a longer look at the old man in the big coat. He had heard of Captain Jack's exploits in his younger days as a buffalo hunter for the railroad on the Texas plains, feared by owlhoots on both sides of the Rio Grande. He didn't look his image now, bowed-backed in the saddle, face drawn and grey grizzled, coloured only by the redness of blood on his right cheek.

Then, Garrett thought, it was downright unkind of him to think such disparaging thoughts about the captain. He had no need to pass judgement on a fellow peace officer. A bunch of murderous kids were running him ragged, making him the laughing stock of Lincoln County. The captain had to have been good at his trade to have stayed alive so long. Boot Hills all over the South-west had graves of badge-toting men who had died young, and violently.

'We had better get the captain down from his

horse before he falls off,' he said. 'You see to his wound, young miss, me and you, boy, will plant the late Johnny Bear.'

The four of them were sitting round the fire, the captain's hands gripping a hot mug of coffee, laced with a generous shot of Pat Garrett's whiskey on the insistence of the marshal that suffering a severe blow on the head as he had, he needed a pick-me-up. The captain felt mentally strong enough to know that it wouldn't start him off on another wild drinking session, but he had glanced at Floyd and Belle, hangdog like, letting them know he wasn't backsliding, wasn't weakening in his resolve to clear Ketch and his gang off their property.

Belle sweet-smiled and gave him a slight nod of understanding. Only then did he hold out his mug for Garrett to pour him out a shot of whiskey. Garrett kept having the occasional pull at the bottle as he listened intently as Floyd told him of the cattle-lifting that was being carried out in this corner of Lincoln County, and how he had asked Captain Jack to come and help him and Belle to stamp it out.

'Now Ketch and his gang have joined up with Billy the Kid's men, Mr Garrett,' Floyd said, 'to hunt down the captain. That's why me and Belle are campin' out here, to warn the captain what odds he's facing. We were goin' to tell him to head back to Presido before he got himself killed, that me and Sis would fend for ourselves from now on in.'

Captain Jack spat disconsolately into the fire. 'I reckon I oughta get myself back to Texas,' he growled. 'Allowin' a no-good 'breed to come a-sneakin' up on me.'

'There's no need to fret over that, Captain,' Garrett said, consolingly. 'Johnny Bear was the best there was in Indianing-up on folk unexpectedly like. So Billy and his boys are in Artesia, eh? It would be just my blamed luck to find where they are when I'm on my own. My deputies are scattered all over the county trying to cut Billy's sign. If he catches sight of me riding into Artesia he'll scoot, then I've lost him again.'

'It ain't been a wasted ride, Pat,' Captain Jack said. 'You saved three lives and killed a real bad-ass, and I'm beholden to you.' He favoured Pat with a lopsided smile. 'M'be I'll get to pay you back sometime.'

'The way I read it, Capt'n,' Garrett said, 'Billy's letting the 'breed do the hard work, him and his boys will be in Artesia, and Ketch and his gang will be at your place, Floyd. Between them they're trying to corral you in, Capt'n.' Garrett grinned. 'I figure we should do some hemming in of our own. Ketch won't be expecting any trouble and if there's only five of them, and one's already winged, it'll be no sweat to winkle 'em out. That will solve your problem, Floyd.' Garrett's grin grew colder. 'Mine will take a mite longer to clear up.'

'Yeah, I reckon me and you could do that easy enough, Marshal,' Captain Jack replied. 'Only that could mean us shootin' lumps out of the kids' home. Ketch ain't goin' to come out willingly.'

'There's no need for either of you to risk your lives on our behalf,' Floyd said. 'Me and Belle have decided to quit the place, make a new start at Fort Sumner. We intend burning the house down before we leave.'

'Burn it down!' the captain cried, spilling his coffee as he jerked upright. 'Why your pa and ma musta sweated blood buildin' it! It's your home!'

'I know they did, Capt'n,' replied Floyd. 'And I don't want yours or Mr Garrett's blood spilt savin' it. Me and Belle couldn't live in it with that price tag hangin' over our heads.' Floyd's face steeled over. 'And Uncle Slater ain't goin' to live in it.'

Mumbling to himself that he hadn't hard-assed it all the way from Presido to quit a fight that had hardly started, the captain got to his feet. 'I'll take a stroll. I can think better when I'm movin' around.' He beady-eyed Floyd. 'But one thing I'm sure about, boy, we're a long ways from doin' any burnin' down.'

The captain stepped out of the brush to have a clear view of the flat. The whiskey-laced coffee had settled his nerves somewhat allowing him to do some deep thinking. He believed the tall lawman was right, placing Billy the Kid and his wild boys in Artesia. If somehow they could be persuaded that this part of Lincoln County was

decidedly unhealthy for them, the captain
thought, that would leave Ketch and his gang
isolated. Ketch would have to come out and do his
own tracking to find him. And Ketch, he opined,
was no Johnny Bear. The captain grinned. He
would have regained his lost edge here on the flat.
He would have the West Texas sons-of-bitches
shooting at their own shadows.

The stumbling block to his grand plan was how
the hell was he going to get Billy the Kid ass-kicking it out of Artesia, or put where he could do no
more harm, like dead, or in the jailhouse? In the
far distance his gaze caught the sight of a long,
slow-moving dust-haze. Chisum's longhorns had
started their trail northwards. A sudden smile
eased the worry lines on his face. Chisum's cows
had helped him out the first time, could they be
his ace-in-the-hole again? He turned and hurried
back to the camp.

Marshal Garrett looked at him expectantly as
he came up to the fire.

'Marshal,' he said, 'I think I've come up with a
plan that oughta catch Billy the Kid off guard,
kinda confuse him, so givin' us the chance of plug-
gin' him and some of his boys. Leastways it should
send him runnin' scared and keep him from liftin'
Chisum's cows for a spell. And it will leave Ketch
and his gang where I want them, on their own,
frettin' about how many hunters are closin' in on
him.'

'Confuse . . . running scared . . . Mr Bonney?'

said an incredulous-faced Garrett. 'He's the sonuvabitch who does all the confusing and scaring. He's got me and my deputies running all over the county like a bunch of headless chickens!'

Captain Jack grinned. 'Believe me, Marshal, young Billy will be more than a mite confused and scared, he'll be in one helluva panic when a hundred or so stampedin' longhorns are bearin' down on him and his boys in that broken-down shack that passes for a bar in Artesia.'

'And I suppose you have longhorns you speak of at hand,' Garrett said, making the effort to keep the sarcasm out of his voice.

'Yeah, more or less,' replied the captain. 'I've picked up the dust of a herd of Chisum's cows headin' this way. His straw boss will be with them. If I can sweet-talk him into lettin' us borrow, so to speak, a sizeable chunk of the herd then I've got a plan. I figure he should be willin' to oblige us when he knows we're goin' to use them against the Kid who's regularly liftin' his boss's cattle.'

Garrett sat pondering for a while. He had heard of some crazy plans in his life but the old Ranger's took the prize. Though if it got him within rifle range of the Kid who was he to call it wild? He stood up, his lips twitching in the ghost of a smile.

'Capt'n,' he said, 'I've heard better plans, but that don't mean this mad-hat scheme of yours won't work. Though we had better get it moving and catch up with those cows you need before they're pushed across the Pecos. The trail-hands won't feel like obliging you if it means getting the cattle back on this side of the river.' He turned to face Floyd. 'You can keep Johnny Bear's horse and gear, boy,' he said. 'He'll have no further use of them where he's bound for.' He smiled. 'The 'breed's pistol will be a mite more reliable than that old cannon you're sporting if you have to face a man with anger in your heart again.'

'Let's go then, Marshal,' Captain Jack said. He gave Floyd and Belle a stern-faced fatherly look. 'You stay here and keep out of sight in case any of Ketch's gang come by. But I promise you this, Floyd, if it is possible, when the final reckonin' comes with your uncle, you'll be in on it, OK?'

'OK, Capt'n,' replied Floyd.

Floyd watched the two veteran lawmen ride out towards the nearing herd with mixed feelings. He sighed. It was getting to be a dangerous, complicated business ousting Uncle Slater from the holding. He and Belle could yet be making the trip to Fort Sumner with the smoke of their burning home in their nostrils.

TWELVE

Billy the Kid, sitting at a table in Artesia's bar, gnawed savagely at his left thumb. He didn't like staying too long in any given location, unless it was a Mexican village where he had *amigos*, goat and sheep-tenders on the outskirts of the village who would come running in to warn him of approaching riders. Marshal Pat Garrett, who had the dogged patience of an Indian, had made it his life's work to hunt him down. And Billy knew that a man couldn't go on killing and rustling until he was a ripe old age. *Hombres* died young, and sudden, by the bullet or the rope in that dangerous business. The law, when it came down to it, Billy was well aware, had all the edge.

'Any signs of the 'breed yet, Dave?' he called out through the open door.

'Naw!' Dave yelled back, lounging in the shade of the porch acting as look-out. 'Ain't any signs of anything or anyone movin' this side of the Pecos.'

'It'll be a while before Johnny Bear shows up,

Billy,' Sam Clancy said. He was sitting on the opposite side of the table shuffling a greasy, dog-eared pack of cards. 'He ain't got an easy task tryin' to track down a sneaky sonuvabitch regulator. Place your bets, Kid, I feel lucky.' And he began dealing out the cards.

'Yeah, I suppose so,' mumbled a disgruntled Billy. 'But it's not knowin' where the long *hombre* is that's got me chawin' at my nails.' He grinned at Clancy. 'When the 'breed brings in Ketch's regulator I'll promise him another coupla bottles of snake juice to track down and plug Pat Garrett.'

'The look-out kid is Dave Ridaburgh, Capt'n,' Garrett said. 'If Billy's got his full gang here there'll be another six, counting Billy, inside. The horses will be tied up at the back of the bar.'

'Dave don't look old enough to have partaken in any serious law-breakin',' the captain said.

'Billy's even younger,' replied Garrett. 'But don't let their altar-boy looks fool you, they're as wild a band of outlaws who have ever ridden across the State of New Mexico, or any other territory for that matter. Do not hesitate to shoot to kill when Chisum's cows open up the ball. They can only come out by that door or the two windows.'

The captain gave Garrett a hard-faced look. 'I'll do what is necessary, Marshal, to get Billy outa my hair. If that means killin' so be it.' His face had the stoic expression of a man who took fate as it came, but inside he was worried sick that the Jingle Bob crew had promised him more than they could deliver. He made himself more comfortable behind the slight ridge, overlooking the bar in Artesia as patiently as he could, the Henry fully loaded.

The pair of them had met up with Chisum's herd before it had reached the Pecos and the captain explained to Brady, who was riding with the point men, the need for the use of some of his cows for a short time.

Brady sat back in his saddle, a disbelieving look twisting his face. He took off his hat and scratched his head. 'Am I hearin' you right, Capt'n? I ain't got a touch of the sun? You did say you wanted me to arrange a stampede? Christ, Mr Chisum will have my balls if I don't get these cows across the river before dark!'

Captain Jack grinned at the straw boss. 'Mr Chisum might look more kindly on you if he knows that a bunch of his longhorns helped to rope in Billy the Kid and his gang. Or at least have them ass-kickin' it well clear of the Jingle Bob range.'

'Billy the Kid!' Brady spluttered. 'That young hellion!' He rammed his hat back on to his head. 'Why the old man will give me a raise if we got Billy dead or long ways from here. Tell me more about this stampede you want. But I'd better get some of my crew up here first so they can help your plan. They'll have to handle the stampede.'

A shut-faced Brady only grunted now and again as the captain told him of how he and Garrett intended to catch the Kid when he was least expecting an attack on him. 'Can your boys do it without Billy suspectin' any trouble till the cows are snortin' down his neck? You're the experts.'

'What do you think, Juan?' said Brady.

The *vaquero* grinned at Captain Jack and Marshal Garrett. 'We "greasers" always thought you *gringos* were *loco*, but I reckon we can do it. There's a wide dry arroyo leadin' right up to Artesia. Billy won't even see their dust till they come boilin' out of the wash. Though it can only be a hundred and fifty or so cows, *Capitan*. We can't handle any more if we have to move them fast and keep it quiet.'

Captain Jack matched his grin. 'That'll do fine, *greaser*, he said. 'My Henry and the Marshal's Winchester will do the rest. We don't want any of you trail-hands mixed up in the shootin' or Mr Chisum will be hollerin' for me and Marshal Garrett's balls.'

'There's no chance of that,' Brady growled. 'They'll have their work cut out turnin' the herd to bring 'em back here. Take old Red with you, Juan.' Brady looked at Captain Jack. 'He's the meanest longhorn on the range. When his dander's up he'll stomp every shack in Artesia into kindlin'.'

'Me and Marshal Garrett will head for Artesia,' Captain Jack said. 'And get ourselves set for takin' on Billy and his bunch.' He nodded to Juan. 'I'll be really lookin' forward to seein' old Red come fire-ballin' in with his harem.'

Dave pricked up his ears and stepped to the edge of the porch and looked skywards quizzically. He had thought he had heard thunder yet the sky was one cloudless blue arc clear away to the mountains. The thunder became louder and Dave became more puzzled as he reckoned he could also hear high-pitched yells among the thunder rolls. Then, as if sprouting from the ground, he saw a line of bobbing, bellowing, dust-raising shapes appear in front of his eyes.

'Holy cow!' he gasped and stepped back to the door, yelling inside, 'It's a stampede, Billy! Headin' this way! Let's get the hell out of it before they spook our horses!'

Garrett thin-smiled at Captain Jack. 'Big Red has given us the break we wanted let's not let the critter down.'

He fired first and an invisible hand pushed Dave through the doorway, arms failing as if trying to regain his balance. Choking on his own blood from a deadly lung shot, he fell headlong into the bar. For a split-second, Billy and the rest of the gang, on hearing Dave's warning, and witnessing his sudden killing, had been frozen in time. Then the shaking of the shack by the vibrations of hundreds of pounding hooves closing fast across the hard-pan settlement brought them all back to life again. Clancy was the first to move. He flung his cards down on to the table and made a dash for the nearest window as the stampeding herd roared past.

Clancy saw several wild-eyed longhorns heading for the bar porch and hurriedly drew himself back into the bar. Captain Jack's single shot, fired almost blindly through the dust-haze, caught Clancy in the left arm, causing him to lose his grip on the window frame and fall outwards on to the porch. He managed one terrified scream before the cows, bringing down the porch roof and shattering the floor planking, stamped him into a broken bundle of bloody flesh and bones.

In less than a minute the cattle had stormed past Artesia leaving the buildings looking as though they had been hit by a twister. Captain Jack took a quick look in the slowly settling dust-clouds and not seeing any trail-hands following the cows in, emptied the magazine of the Henry at the door and windows in one non-stop burst.

Billy, crouched under the table, cursed a blue streak as shells ripped through the rotting wood of the shack, punching holes in the back adobe wall that sent showers of jagged-edged lumps of plaster hurtling across the bar as painfully flesh-slashing as a bursting canister shell.

Billy quickly began to assess how bad things were for him. As bad as they could be, he opined, with Garrett out front. Dave was spread out in front of him well on his way to Hell, and he didn't like to think of how fearfully Sam had died. He could hear Tom Pickett moaning as though he had been hit real bad. Then the rapid-firing son-of-a-bitch opened up again at them. They were definitely between a rock and a hard place. It was crow-eating time.

'Garrett!' he yelled above the noise. 'What the hell have you got out there, a blasted Gatling gun?'

'I've got six of Mr Chisum's wild-ass drovers with me, Billy,' lied Garrett. 'They've stayed behind to finish off what they started. They've already picked out the tree you and what's left of your boys are going to swing from. What's left of Clancy will have to scraped up off the dirt and put in a burlap sack.'

If it hadn't already been demonstrated, bursting their way out, guns blazing, would be suicidal. Billy gave vent to his anger and fear by dirty-mouthing Garrett.

'There's no need to get bad-tempered, Billy,' Garrett shouted back. 'You have to take the rough with the smooth. Though I'm willing to offer you a deal!'

'What deal's that, Pat?' replied Billy, thinking that any deal that left him alive was much better than getting shot to pieces.

'If you all throw your guns out of the window,' Garrett said, 'and walk out on to the street, hands grabbing at air, I'll escort you to Fort Sumner to stand trial in front of a judge and jury. I ain't promising you they won't sentence you to be hanged, but at least it'll give you time to plead your case up as far as Governor Wallace. All the time you'll get from the trail-hands here is a few minutes to say your prayers before they lash your horse from under you. Think on it, Billy, but not too long!' Garrett nodded to Captain Jack. 'Put a few more lead persuaders about their ears, Capt'n.'

Captain Jack put the reloaded Henry to his shoulder and squeezed the trigger. Another fusillade of shells tore into the shack.

Before the echoes of the barrage had died away they both heard Billy's cry of, 'We're quittin' Pat! No more shootin'! We're comin' out with our hands held high. I'm trustin' you to hold off Chisum's crew!'

Garrett grinned at the captain. 'Billy was never any good at playing poker.'

'Some kids get ideas well above their capabilities, Marshal, and it leads them to an early grave,' the captain replied, as he thumbed fresh shells into the rifle's loading tube.

They saw rifles and pistols being thrown out of the windows, then Billy, hands raised high, one of them holding a piece of once-white cloth, stepped out on to the porch, followed by two of his gang, one with a bloodied face.

'Tom Pickett's back there, sorely wounded, Pat,' Billy said.

'You two boys go back in then and bring him out,' Garrett said. 'You just stay where I can see you, Billy.'

Billy gazed nervously about him then he gave out a gasp. 'Why you sonuvabitch, Pat, you bluffed me! You ain't got anyone backin' you up but that old goat!' He looked at Captain Jack in surprise. 'Why, you're the old *hombre* who passed through here the other day.' Then he noticed the piercing-eyed, Indian-faced visage of a man who wasn't all old, and the Henry rifle held steady on him. Something clicked inside Billy's head. He grinned. 'And you're the sonuvabitch who's got Ketch all het up!' Billy narrow-eyed the captain. 'I reckon Johnny Bear won't be ridin' this way again.'

The captain shook his head. 'Not unless he passes this way makin' his way to Hell. As you surely will, boy, if you so much as give me an unkind look.'

Billy's grin faded away fast as he looked at the captain. The old goat, he thought, had the most unnerving gaze he had ever seen coming from a white man. He and Garrett had been *amigos* once, still were as friendly as a lawman and an outlaw could be. The tall man, he knew, would let him have some rope. The only rope he would get from the old man would be the length that would hang him.

Billy switched his gaze back on to Garrett. 'Tell the old *pistolero* I meant what I said about quitting the fight. Me and my boys will ride in peaceable with you to Fort Sumner.' He turned as the feet-dragging Pickett was being carried out of the bar. 'I ain't leavin' Tom to bleed to death out here.'

'A wise decision, Billy,' Garrett said. 'But Tom will have to be left here, because your horses took off just ahead of the cows so you'll have to walk a piece before you pick them up. If you hadn't loose tied them you'd have to trek it all the way in to Fort Sumner. The women can tend to Tom till we can get the doc out here.'

Garrett swung down from his horse. 'Keep them covered, Captain Jack,' he said, 'till I tie their hands. A rope is a stronger binding than a man's word. Then I'll roust out some of the whores to look after Tom.'

'Captain Jack!' exclaimed Billy, favouring the captain with another close-eyed look. 'I've heard old Mexes relate tales about a Captain Jack of the Texas Rangers. Wiped out a whole passel of rustlers single-handed in old Mexico, so the story went.'

'I was as wild as you those days, boy,' Captain Jack said. 'Though on the side of the law.' Then Billy got another glimpse of the captain's off-putting gaze. 'Another thing you ought to know about me is that I've personal business to settle up with Ketch. Now I ain't interested in what may or may not happen to you at Fort Sumner, but I'll tell you this, *amigo*, if I get you in the sights of my Henry again you're dead, *comprende*?'

Billy managed to show his boyish grin. 'Captain

Jack, Ketch ain't actually an *amigo* of mine,' he said. 'More like kind of a business pard. And it looks like that business is folded up. In any case Ketch is big enough to fight his own battles.' And lose them for sure, Billy said, under his breath.

'Will you be OK, Marshal, takin' them in on your own?' Captain Jack said.

Pat Garrett was up on his horse tying the end of the lead rope to his saddle-horn. His three prisoners, hands tied behind backs, were stretched out in a line behind him, sour-faced, looking at the prospect of a long, hot walk. Two of Artesia's played-out, short-time women had helped Pickett back into the saloon, having been paid by Billy more than they could earn in a week plying their lewd trade, to see to the wounded man's needs.

'Yeah, I'll be fine,' Garrett replied. 'These boys ain't gonna cause me any bother, they gave me their word.' He jerked hard on the rope, almost pulling his captives off their feet. 'And they know they can either walk or be dragged to Fort Sumner. Are you sure you'll be OK, Capt'n? If you hold off from what you intend doing to rope in Ketch and his gang till I see these *hombres* behind bars I'll swing back this way and give you a hand. I owe you that for helping me catch Billy.'

Captain Jack grinned. 'I ain't figured out yet how I'm goin' to tackle the Texan hard-cases. And by what I hear you've got a war goin' on in your territory, you'll have your work cut out as a peace officer to try and keep a lid on it. You've done enough to reduce the odds more than somewhat against me.' He smiled broadly at Garrett's prisoners. 'You boys have a nice trip now.'

The captain pulled his horse round to head back to the Pecos, still smiling until he could no longer hear Billy's and his *compadres* cursing and dirty-mouthing. Then his face lost its humorous lines as he began to ponder over the serious business of honouring his pledge to Floyd and Belle.

THIRTEEN

Captain Jack drew up Stonewall at the foot of a rocky outcrop leading up to an isolated, thick brush-covered ridge. He took out his rifle from its boot then dismounted and picked his way through the rocks until he reached the foot of the ridge. He trod over a heavy deposit of shale and grass and weed-covered heaps of spoil, pushing aside clumps of brush until he gave a grunt of satisfaction. He had found what he had been seeking: the entrance into the abandoned mine.

He stood at the dark opening for several seconds, sniffing, the Henry held ready for action across his waist, in case the cave-like shaft was a big cat's lair. Satisfied that no animal or man had entered the mine since the day its owners quit breaking their backs looking for the motherlode, he walked inside.

The captain paused again until his eyes adjusted to the darkness and he could see that the shaft took a sharp right turn. He continued on the few yards to the bend then found out that several more yards in, an old roof fall had completely blocked the shaft.He gave another pleased grunt. The place was ideal for Floyd and Belle. The horses could be tethered, well hidden among the rocks. The only drawback was that fresh water would have to be taken fron a small stream a couple of hundred yards across the flat.

He didn't know how long it would take to get the better of Ketch and his gang; too long, he knew, for Floyd and his sister to stay in an unsheltered camp on a cold, wind-swept plain. Plus the added risk of the rustlers stumbling on to the camp. Here a fire could be lit without being seen from the outside, and could be used to hold any prisoners he may take. The captain opined the kids would get the feeling they were helping him to regain their property standing guard over a prisoner. Though already Floyd had shown his willingness to fight for his birthright by standing up to the 'breed armed with his pa's old relic of a pistol.

The captain came down from the mine and remounted Stonewall, taking one last look at the ridge before riding off, making sure his probing about for the way in hadn't exposed the mine entrance. Then, digging his heels lightly into Stonewall's ribs, he set off in a ground-eating trot to Floyd's camp.

Belle, on watch, pulled the blanket tighter about her shoulders. The wind, blowing from the north,

had a bone-chilling bite to it. Floyd sat at the fire,
Johnny Bear's .44 Colt in pieces on his knees,
ready to be assembled after being cleaned and
oiled and the action checked. His neglect in checking on the Walker had almost cost him his life and
Marshal Garrett wouldn't be riding by a second
time to save it again.

'I've found a warmer spot for you to make camp,
Floyd,' he suddenly heard Captain Jack say from
behind him. Startled, he twisted round spilling
the pistol parts on to the ground to look up at the
captain in wide-eyed surprise. How the heck had
he come through the brush, rein-leading his horse
without him or Belle hearing him, he wondered.
Floyd shivered. It could have been Ketch or any of
his men sneaking in on them. He always seemed
to be letting himself down in front of the captain,
Floyd thought, despondently.

The captain looked about him. 'Where's your
sister, Floyd?' he asked. Then suffered a nervous
twitch or two himself on hearing Belle say, 'I'm
right behind you, Captain Jack. I heard you
coming in and I thought it could have been one of
the rustlers. If I had shouted out a warning to
Floyd he would have known he could no longer
surprise us and start firing.' Belle smiled self-
consciously. 'So I did some Indian-walking myself.'

'You did the right thing, Miss Belle,' the captain
said. Then, looking at her closely, he added, 'Do
you think you could have pulled the trigger on
that rifle you're totin' if I had been a rustler?'

'I think so', Captain,' Belle replied, hesitantly. Then, face all bone, she said, 'If it had been Palmer I wouldn't have thought twice before I fired.'

'Good for you, missy,' Captain Jack said. 'Always remember that yours and Floyd's lives come before those of Ketch and his gang. They wouldn't hesitate in killin' you both if it suited their purpose. Now let's get this camp broke up and get settled into the new one before it gets dark. I'll tell you how things came our way at Artesia on the ride there.'

Floyd cast admiring glances at his sister as he rolled up their blankets. He was proud that his sister had proved to the captain that they would be no hindrance to him, but good allies in the fight against the rustlers.

FOURTEEN

A scowling-faced Ketch stood on the porch gazing into nowhere, his mind too occupied to have noticed a Comanche war party if they had come hollering up to the house. Something, he sensed, had gone wrong, badly wrong.

He had hoped by now he would have had news from Billy that Johnny Bear had tracked down the regulator, or whoever it was causing them the trouble. Then the lucrative rustling deal he and the Kid had going between them could start up again. The losing of the latest bunch of Chisum's cows, the killing of Hackett he had accepted as the occasional upsets in the hazardous trade of cattle-lifting. The gut-twisting feeling he was getting right now had him thinking that things were going to get a lot worse for him here in Lincoln County. Muttering curses, Ketch walked back inside the house.

Slater was sitting at the table, hitting the bottle hard, face looking as though he was gazing into

117

his own grave. Ketch reckoned the sodbuster was
reading the signs the way he was. He gave him a
cutting look. 'You want to go easy downin' that
rotgut,' he said. 'Big trouble could be headin' this
way and we'll need every gun we can muster.' All
he got from Slater was drunken-mouthed curses.
There and then, he decided, if they had to make a
run for it, he would personally plug the chicken-
livered son-of-a-bitch dead, and send the two kids
following their uncle if they got in his way.

Ketch swore, then got a grip on his depressing
thoughts. He would be damned if he was going to
stand here waiting for trouble to come knocking
at the porch door. 'Cal!' he shouted. 'Get mounted
up and ride to Artesia and ask Billy how that
tracker of his is makin' out! By all the dust we've
been seein' these past coupla days Chisum's
movin' a lot of his cattle north. I want a few
hundred or more head of them before all the cows
left on the Jingle Bob range are pulled close to the
damned big house outa Billy's reach.'

It was a highly nervous Cal who rode along the
trail to Artesia. He was thinking that the son-of-
a-bitch who had downed poor Hackett and winged
Pike could be hunkered down behind any patch of
brush or fold in the ground ready to back-shoot
him as he passed by. He hadn't mentioned that
fear to Ketch when he had told him to ride to
Artesia. To have done so would have been inviting
sudden death. Ketch was a tetchy *hombre* on good
days, and the last days had been anything but

good at all for the gang. If he had started to complain about the trip Ketch would have gut-shot him.

Maybe, he thought hopefully, the regulator would take him for a Jingle Bob ranch-hand out lookin for strays. That reasoning eased Cal's fear somewhat. Though not enough to ease the painful itchy feeling in his back at the fearful prospect of it being a target of a killing rifle shell.

Captain Jack, on seeing the rider through his army glass, took him to be one of Chisum's cowhands until he headed towards Artesia. He gave a grim smile. Things were better than he had hoped. Ketch was feeling the pressure. And a man knowing he was being pushed into a corner often makes wild and careless moves, like sending one of his boys out on his ownsome to Artesia to see how Billy's plan to track Jack down was making out, a man Captain Jack would make sure Ketch would lose, either as his prisoner, or, if he chose the hard way when the time came, dead.

He had seen Floyd and Belle settled down in their new camp. The canteens had been filled from the stream and he had seen to it that the horses were fed and watered and bedded down, corralled among the rocks. He had told Floyd and Belle there was thus no need for them to leave the safety of the mine.

'We've got the edge over Ketch and his gang,' he said to them. 'Let's not throw it away by showin' ourselves to him before we're good and ready to take him on. I know you're itchin' to play your full part in the fight, Floyd, but just curb your impatience till I've cut the odds against us some more. Now I'm goin' out to scout around to try and find out what Ketch's next moves are.' He grinned at them both. 'If I get lucky I could be bringin' you back a prisoner to guard.'

Now it looked as though his luck was in; the kids would get their man to guard. He walked back to Stonewall, tethered in a nearby dip in the ground, to ride closer to the trail and fix up a surprise meeting with Ketch's man when he returned from Artesia with his head spinning with the bad news for his boss he would hear there.

Cal's horse came back along the trail raising the dust high. Cal lashing at its ass with the reins like an old-time Pony Express courier. He had been worried on his way to Artesia, but on being told that Pat Garrett and an old Texas Ranger captain wearing a tent of a coat, helped for Christ's sake, by a bunch of stampeding cattle, had roped in Billy the Kid and his gang, killing two of his boys for good measure, Cal was downright, bowel-looseningly scared. The tall man had taken Billy and his boys back to the jailhouse at Fort Sumner, which meant the old captain was still out here someplace. Texas Rangers were hard, mean-thinking men, and the justice they dished out was as swift and final as any hired

bounty hunter or regulators. His wild thoughts
about a rustler-hunter being behind any brush or
ridge wasn't so way out now.

Then he had to tell Ketch the bad news. He
would laugh his head off thinking he was joshing
him. When it finally sunk in it was true, Ketch
would shoot him. It would be a wise decision for
him to ride hell-for-leather for the Pecos and the
Panhandle. Cal was almost in tears on how fast
his luck had taken a nose-dive. His high-spending
days were gone; staying alive was all that
mattered. He dug his spurs savagely into his
horse's ribs, urging it to greater speed, all the
while keen-eying both sides of the trail with the
nervous itch in his back playing him up again.

Just when he was beginning to breathe a little
easier putting more miles between him and the
danger zone around Artesia, Cal's luck took the
final plunge to rock bottom. The old Ranger
captain, up on his horse, was in the middle of the
trail, like some Indian chief with his big coat
wrapped around him.

Face twisted in fear and anger, Cal jerked hard
on the bit, bringing his horse into a hoof-sliding
halt. He knew he had only one option, to stand
and fight. It was kill or be killed time, by the
bullet right here, or by the rope later, unless he
could outshoot the hard-eyeing old bastard ahead
of him.

Captain Jack saw Cal's mad-eyed look of
desperation that told him he wasn't about to get

himself a prisoner. His right hand holding the Henry swept upwards from behind the skirt of his coat, dropping the barrel across his left forearm, firing it between Stonewall's ears.

Cal gave out a gasping grunt of pain and rocked in his saddle as the close-range shot caved in his rib cage. Blood, thick and dark, streamed out of his mouth as he slumped forward across his horse's neck. By the time the captain had calmed down Stonewall and kneed him alongside Cal, the rustler was dead.

'Pilgrim,' he said, dispassionately, 'I was hopin' I'd be able to take you alive so you'd tell me what Ketch's next moves are, but you proved you'd rather die than help a lawman.' The captain grinned. 'Well your luck's still runnin' against you for I think I can use you to my advantage even though you're dead.'

FIFTEEN

Ketch was all worked up inside. Cal was long overdue riding back from Artesia and he was getting an ominous feeling that the regulator, or whoever, had hit him again. It could be, he thought, hopefully, though briefly, that Cal was spending some extra time in Artesia humping some whore, but Cal hadn't been too happy having to ride out and see Billy and he wouldn't risk his neck any longer than he had to in regulator territory, not even for the youngest and prettiest whore in the whole of New Mexico, if she was plying her trade in Artesia.

Cal, Ketch was convinced, wouldn't be showing up this side of Hell. Somewhere along the trail he had met up with the regulator. He pondered over another disturbing thought: if he was right about Cal's fate then where was Billy's crack trail reader? Could he be meeting up with Cal in Hell? The sneaky son-of-a-bitch was picking them off one by one. For the first time in his life Ketch experienced real fear.

Ketch's mind did, however, clutch at one grain of comfort. The regulator must be on his own. If there had been a bunch of them, knowing how many of his gang he had left, they would have come shooting their way in. He glanced out of the window apprehensively, into the fast growing darkness of the night, and turned down the wick of the big lantern hanging from the ceiling above his head. The bastard could be anywhere, he thought, and until he came up with some plan to trap him there was no need to give him any more edge than he had already by presenting him with an easy target.

'Put that light up, Jake,' Palmer said, sitting at the table cleaning his pistols. Then he noticed Ketch's disturbed look. 'You're figurin' the bastard's got Cal, ain't you?'

Ketch nodded slightly. 'And also that part Injun tracker Billy promised us. The son-of-a-bitch is cornerin' us in, Palmer.'

Palmer got up from the table and buckled on his gunbelt. He twirled his two pistols by the trigger guard several times in a flashing blur of movement before slipping them into their fancy fringed sheaths. His smile was as heart warming as a hungry wolf's bared-fang snarl as he tapped the kill notches on the bone butts of the pistols.

'Mister Regulator is as good as dead if he gets within range of these two beauties,' he said.

That display made Ketch more confident he could fight off the unseen deadly threat ranged against him and his gang. The gun-crazy Palmer would take on the Devil in a gunfight, laughing fit to burst doing so. And there was Pike, who had a special grudge against the regulator, Hackett had been a blood cousin of his and being wounded and all by him. He would fight back if it would save his neck from being stretched by the hangman. Slater, slumped in a drunken stupor in the chair by the fire, couldn't be relied on. He had already marked him down for a bullet. Then Ketch had a sudden thought. Maybe Slater could be of some use after all. If Cal didn't show up within the hour he would put his new plan to the test.

'Get the horses on to the front porch, Palmer,' he said. 'Where we can keep an eye on them. We don't want the regulator to drive them off. Keep a watch outside, Pike, while he's bringing them round.'

Pike got to his feet and drew out his pistol. His wounded arm prevented him from handling a rifle. He wasn't too happy at the way things were shaping up for the gang. How the hell, he thought, could he reload his pistol with a busted arm if it came to a gunfight? Yet the alternative was even worse. On his own if he met up with the regulator he would end up dead like Hackett and as he believed, Cal was. No sir, Pike told himself, if it came to a shoot-out the wild-ass *pistolero*, Palmer was the *hombre* to be standing alongside. He followed his possible lifesaver out on to the porch to stand a wide-eyed watch while Palmer brought the horses from the barn.

It was fully dark when Captain Jack, rope-leading Cal's horse with its late owner strapped across its back, approached the house. He drew up well clear of the building, arming himself with the Henry but staying in the saddle, ready for a quick hightail retreat if things turned nasty. He had to consider the possibility that Ketch would have one of his men prowling around the perimeter of the holding.

He saw the horses on the porch and the dimmed lanterns in the house. Ketch and his boys were on edge, he opined. He didn't think their dead *compadre* showing up on the porch would finally convince the gang that it was time for them to quit the rustling business and leave the holding. He was hoping that losing his men one by one would goad Ketch into action to save his face as a gang leader. Ketch would be real mad, and mad-thinking men tend to get careless in their actions. And he would be close by to take hold of any advantage that came his way.

Three faces lit up somewhat at the sound of a horse coming up to the house. Things weren't as bad as they had been thinking. Cal hadn't been shot. And their fears that a regulator could be hovering around outside had only been nervous thinking on their part.

Palmer, standing near a window, looked out at the horse stamping its feet in the dirt in front of the porch. His puzzled gasp of, 'Why, Cal ain't up on his horse, Ketch!' darkened faces with fear again.

Ketch stepped up to the window and took a longer look out. He swore savagely. 'Cal's lyin' across its back! Cover me!' he snapped.

Palmer's twin pistols flashed into his hands. With a quick flick of one wrist he shattered the window with the muzzle of one of his guns, clearing his field of fire. He thumbed back the hammers then bared his teeth in a joyous grin at Ketch signifying he was ready. He waited until Ketch's hand was on the door latch before emptying the full loads of both Colts in one rattling, flame-streaked burst of fire.

Then Ketch was back in the house with Cal's body laid across his shoulder with the echoing of the firing still ringing round the holding. Banging the door shut behind him with the heel of a boot, he laid the body on the table gaunt-faced with cold hatred.

'How many more of us are we goin' to let the sonuvabitch take before we do something about it, Jake?' Palmer asked, looking at the body, as he deftly reloaded his pistols.

Ketch swung round on him and an alarmed Palmer snapped shut the cylinder of the pistol he was loading. Ketch was a hair-triggered-tempered *hombre* and he was capable of gunning him down for daring to question his tactics as the boss man. But he would be damned if he was just going to sit on his ass and let Ketch gun him down. He would do some shooting himself.

'We ain't takin' any more, Palmer,' Ketch said in a calmer voice than he was feeling. 'We're goin' out to look for the sonuvabitch, as we should have done after he killed Hackett, instead of relyin' on Billy the Kid's 'breed tracker.' He cold smiled. 'Wake up that drunken sodbuster; he don't know it but he's gonna help us to get clear of this place just in case the regulator's skulkin' out there.'

The gunfire and the retrieving of the dead rustler's body only strengthened Captain Jack's opinion that Ketch and his boys weren't cowering scared in some corner. It looked as though he still had a fight on his hands. He pulled Stonewall's head round and rode to a stretch of high ground, further away from the house but with a clear view of the rear of the building. He hadn't seen any of Ketch's men patrolling the holding but if he was in Ketch's position he would be sending a man out by the hatch of the root cellar to scout around looking for whoever had sent the dead man in on his last ride. The captain grinned. If he kept his eyes and ears alert he could get himself another scalp.

'Me and the boys are pullin' out, Slater,' Ketch lied. 'We're headin' back to the Panhandle. The rustlin' business we had goin' between us is all washed up. My advice to you is to get your ass to

Fort Sumner, well away from here when the regulator and Chisum's crew come boilin' in hopin' to rope in me and my boys.'

Slater didn't answer him. He was gazing, wide-eyed at Cal's body, sobering up rapidly.

'The regulator won't figure you as a rustler if he stops you on the trail,' Ketch continued. 'Not when he sees you're only armed with a varmint rifle and sitting up on a farm horse. You'll make it to Fort Sumner OK.' He didn't tell Slater that the regulator, if he knew his busines, and at least two dead men proved that this one did, he would shoot him first then check out who he had gunned down. While Slater was being stalked, he and his men would be out in the open and the son-of-a-bitch hunter would find himself being the hunted.

Slater was silently cursing the day he took up Ketch's offer of easy money, his liquor fuddled brain trying to work out his chances of leaving this dirt farm alive. His chances were nil if the place was raided by the Jingle Bob men even if Ketch allowed him to step outside with his hands held high yelling that he wanted no part in the fight. The cow-hands would hang him high for consorting with rustlers.

The only way out this mess was to get away as far as possible from this section of the territory as Ketch had said, putting his trust in the regulator seeing him up on an old horse, wearing patched-assed Levis, not mistaking him for anyone but a sodbuster.

He staggered on to his feet. 'Yeah, I reckon I should make myself scarce, Ketch,' he said. He managed a weak grin. 'You know I ain't no *pistolero*; I'd only be a hindrance to you and your boys. I'll pack what gear I can carry then I'll get my horse from the barn.'

The captain stiffened up in his saddle, all alert, as he heard a barn door creak open, then heard the low neighing of a horse. The rustlers' horses were all tied up on the front stoop so he assumed that the man pussy-footing it about down there was the kids' uncle, Slater. It looked like he'd had a bellyful of the rustling business and Ketch had allowed him to ride out.

The captain opined he knew why Ketch had let his partner quit. Ketch was using Slater as a Judas goat. While he was stalking the farmer, he and his boys would be hightailing it for Texas, Ketch, realizing without Billy and his gang, his cattle-lifting days were over in Lincoln County. Which suited him fine. He had come here to clear Slater and the rustlers off the holding, not to kill them all, that was Marshal Garrett's job. Though just to tie up the loose ends, he would catch up with Slater and make him sign a paper stating he no longer had a claim on the farm. Then, the captain reckoned, he had honoured his promise to Floyd and Belle.

The further along the trail from the holding without incident he went, the more Slater felt he had slipped by the killer of Hackett and Cal. Bold enough, to stop off at Artesia and get himself a couple of drinks to settle his nerves after all he had been through. It would be daylight by the time he made it there and he knew that Big Mike, the bar owner, opened up his gin mill at the cock's crow. His customers, mainly men who rode beyond the law, or aimless drifters, kept irregular drinking hours.

Captain Jack put his army glass back into his pack, Slater was playing into his hands, stopping at Artesia. If he'd had to confront him on the trail it could have meant gun play. While he wanted Slater alive so he could legally sign over his right to the holding to the kids, if it came to Slater making a fight of it he might be forced to kill him to save his own neck. Then some smooth-talking lawyer in Fort Sumner would see that the deeds to the holding were passed on to Slater's kinfolk. Sneaking up on him in a bar, the captain thought, would catch Slater off guard.

Slater saw the broken porch of the bar and the bullet-riddled planking and guessed that a minor battle in the Lincoln County war had recently been played out in Artesia. Not that it mattered to him, his part in the county war, aiding and abetting in the stealing of Chisum's cattle, was over.

Slater was on his fourth whiskey, openly smiling as he thought of how he would get the better of his nephew after all. He would spit in the kid's eye for all the hassle he had heaped on him by selling his share of the holding to the highest bidder. He hoped it would be a dirt-farmer with a brood of snotty-nosed kids. He looked up sharply as a thin-faced, grey-stubble-chinned man, wearing a big well-stained coat sat down on the other side of the table.

Slater's smile sickened then died away altogether. He favoured his unexpected guest with a frightened-eyed look. 'I figure you're the *hombre* that my nephew brung up from Texas,' he said. Captain Jack smiled in acknowledgement.

Slater peered drunkenly at the captain for a moment or two then had a sudden wild thought. 'Why, there ain't any regulator operatin' here!' he said. 'You're the bastard who's been shootin' Ketch's boys, ain't you!'

'The very same, *amigo*,' replied the captain, his smile widening.

Slater's liquor-induced bravado made him think that the wizened-faced old man sitting on the other side of the table didn't have the cut of a fierce manhunter. Then, in spite of all the whiskey he had downed, Slater felt a chill of fear in the pit of his stomach. Hackett and Cal, he thought, must have had the same foolish thoughts just before the old bastard gunned them down. Then some of his fake courage returned.

'You've wasted your time ridin' all this way, mister, to help the kids,' he said. 'That whinin' nephew of mine ain't gonna get full ownership of the farm. I'm ridin' to Fort Sumner to sell my share of the property. And you can't tie me in with any cattle-liftin'. Ketch and his boys are long gone by now so you ain't got any proof they were shacked up at my place. What you gonna do to me now?' he sneered. 'Shoot me in front of witnesses, me a hard-workin' farmer?'

A hurt expression crossed Captain Jack's face. 'Why, what made you think I'd do such an uncharitable act?' he said indignantly. 'I ain't one of Ketch's back-shooters: I was an officer of the law, a Texas Ranger. What I intend doin' to you is to hand you over to Mr Chisum for him to hang you,' he said conversationally. 'Now, as you rightly speak, I ain't got any real proof that you dealt in stolen cows from the Jingle Bob, but Mr Chisum will take the word of a Texas Ranger captain if he says that this man or that man is a rustler. Why, John Chisum will unhook his rope from the wall and have his horse saddled up to have himself a hangin' faster than you've been downin' that rotgut in front of you.' The captain let Slater stew over his threat for a few moments before saying, 'Now, if you was to sign a piece of paper statin' that you had given up your part of the farm you could save Mr Chisum makin' that trip.'

Slater's lips twitched nervously, his tough veneer cracking, The cold-eyed son-of-a-bitch wasn't bluffing. Chisum would only need the slightest hint of a man being a rustler and he would be searching for a handy tree. He was being pushed over the brink. If he wanted to stay alive he would have to sign his rights away to the holding. Before he could tell the old man he was willing to accept his deal, Big Mike took a hand in his affairs.

The barkeep recognized the captain as the man with Garrett in the fight with Billy the Kid. The old man had almost shot his place to bits with his rifle. Then there was the damage the stampeding longhorns had done. On top of that, the old bastard was a Texas Ranger, another good reason in his lawless opinion, for putting two loads of buckshot in his dirty hide.

Over Slater's shoulder Captain Jack saw the big, heavily bearded barkeep bend down behind the bar then straighten up holding a shotgun. One of his own hands came out of his coat pocket, fast, fisting a pistol, firing it almost before it had cleared the pocket. Slater flinched and was temporarily blinded and deafened by the closeness of the discharged pistol.

The barkeep let out a high-pitched howl of pain, dropping the shotgun as he clutched at his bloody, mangled right ear. The captain was up on his feet, guns in both hands, one swinging on to the drinkers standing at the bar.

'You've shot my ear off, you sonuvabitch!' the shock-faced barkeep cried, blood now streaming through his fingers and over his shoulder.

'That I have, *amigo*, that I have,' replied Captain Jack. 'And I was aimin' for between your eyes. It just shows you how old I'm gettin'. You just stay put, big man, while I finish my business here with Mr Bishop. No more "Glory Boy" stunts or so help me I'll remove your other ear. And I might get lucky and put another eye in your thick head.'

Between moans, Big Mike cursed the captain to Hell and beyond, but was too fond of his life to try and snatch the shotgun from the floor and have another attempt at shooting the sharp-shooting captain.

'I take it you two boys ain't about to have a hand in this trouble,' the captain said to the two drinkers at the bar, their backs still towards him in spite of the shooting and the painful groans of the barkeep.

One of the men turned, his face the washed-out, red-rimmed-eyed visage of a man partaking of the hair-of-the-dog. He favoured the captain with a squint-eyed look.

'Mister,' he said, 'me and my buddy have all the trouble we can handle tryin' to hold down this rattlesnake piss that big fat slob sells on as drinkin'-man's whiskey. Why, we wouldn't be put out if you blowed his other ear off.' Then he turned back to the bar to continue his drinking.

'Good,' replied the captain. 'I like men who mind their own business, but ain't afraid to speak their view.' He pulled out a piece of crumpled paper and a stub of pencil from the inside pocket of his coat and sat down. Grinning across at the sour-faced Slater, he placed the paper and pencil in front of him.

'Now I know it's only a scrap of paper but it will do. It's not as though we're two warrin' generals signin' some peace treaty or whatever, so we cut out all the wherefore's and whereas's and all that crap.'

The captain waved the pistol under Slater's nose. 'Now get writin', *pronto*, or I might take a likin' to shootin' off *hombres'* ears who upset me. Start off with, "I, Slater Bishop, bein' of sound mind, etc, etc. . . ." Then when you're finished I'll get those two hard-drinkin' gents at the bar to witness it.'

SIXTEEN

Standing barefoot in the stream, Belle bent low and splashed water over her bared breasts and arms. Soon she and Floyd would be back home and she would enjoy the luxury of a long hot soak in the tub. Captain Jack had just returned, ending their night-long worries about the terrible things that could have happened to him being away so long.

She could hardly hold back her tears when she saw his haggard face and slow painful walk as he came up the slope to the cave. She remembered her opinion of him when she had seen him for the first time in Presido and her eyes filled with tears again. How terribly wrong she had been. He had won through for her and Floyd, even had to kill for them. They would never be able to pay him back for all he had done.

'This piece of paper,' he had told them, waving it in his hand as he came into the cave, smiling, 'gives you back your land, Floyd. Slater won't bother you again, neither will Ketch. He and his gang have quit the territory. You can go back to your place any time you want, I'll come with you just to check things out. Though I'd appreciate it if you could put the trip off for a few hours, I could do with some sleep. It's been a long few days and nights for an old *hombre*, I can tell you.'

'We're in no hurry to return to the house, Captain,' she had told him. 'Are we, Floyd? The stock will come to no harm. You rest and I'll have a meal ready for you when you wake up.'

'You better do as she says, Capt'n,' Floyd said. 'Belle always gets her own way.'

Once the captain had fallen asleep she had told Floyd she would go down to the stream and give herself a good wash before preparing a meal for the captain.

The water was cool and refreshing on her body, easing the tensions and stresses that had been within her for so long. She felt settled enough in her mind to plan the alterations to the room Uncle Slater had slept in now the farm really did belong to her and Floyd.

Suddenly Belle saw the vague shimmering outline of a shadow darken the water alongside her. She spun round in embarrassed alarm, hands shielding her bared breasts. Her embarrassment changed to a feeling of pure terror when she saw it was Palmer standing at the edge of the stream, grinning lewdly at her.

She screamed loud her fears and turned to run

downstream, but Palmer was quicker. He grabbed
one of her arms and jerked her out of the water.
Then both his arms were around her, pulling her
tight against him, laughing at her futile attempts
to escape from his clutches. She almost gagged as
she smelt the rancid odour of his body sweat. His
lips were on her cheek then her neck as his hand
reached behind to tear off the rest of her clothes.

Wild with fear, Belle made one last desperate
try to free herself. She wriggled her right hand
round until she could pull out the knife sheathed
on her hip. She still hadn't the freedom of movement to inflict a serious wound on Palmer but she
did manage to slash him across the thigh with the
blade, and get the satisfaction of hearing her
molester cry with pain and release her. Sobbing,
she dropped the knife and took off downstream in
a high foot-splashing run.

'You bitch!' Palmer yelled, and plunged in the
water after her, his hand clutching at his leg. 'I
was goin' to break you in gently. But not any more
I ain't!'

Part blinded by the spray she was kicking up,
Belle ran straight into the arms of Ketch as she
came out of the stream. He lifted her clear of the
ground, kicking and screaming. 'If you don't stop
your strugglin' missy,' he snarled. 'I'll lay my
pistol barrel against your purty little head.'

A petrified Belle looked at the hard, merciless
face. Ketch would maybe not rape her but she
knew with absolute frightening certainty that the

gang leader would kill her if it suited his purpose. She stopped her struggling and Ketch lowered her to the ground, to see a limping Palmer, mouthing obscenities, coming splashing down the stream towards her.

'Leave her be, Palmer!' Ketch snapped. 'She's our bait to get the sonuvabitch who killed Hackett and Cal, and ruined the good thing we had goin' here. After we have him comin' in with his hands held high you can do what you like with her. Touch her before that and I'll plug you, *comprende*?'

Ketch's stone-eyed gaze cut right through Palmer like a knife. He could understand Ketch's concern, though he didn't like it. Before he gave himself up for the girl, the regulator would want to see if she was OK. If he knew she had been forcibly used he would still come in, though shooting. He grabbed the girl roughly by the arm and led her to their camp in the brush, where a grinning Pike took in the exposed firm young breasts. Belle was too numbed on hearing her fate to cover herself up from the lecherous gaze.

Floyd had become so worried about the length of time Belle was taking to have a wash he had gone down to the stream to see what was delaying her return. There was no signs of her on both banks of the stream as far along as he could see. Her coat, shirt and shoes and stockings were on the ground at the spot on the bank where she used to clean the pans. Wondering what could have happened to her he bent down and picked up her clothes, and saw something that chilled his blood, footprints of two men. Booted footprints, so at least she couldn't have been spirited away by Indians. But who? he thought, frantically.

With the sickness of fear biting away at his stomach Floyd sped blindly back to the cave and shook Captain Jack awake, yelling in his ear, 'It's Belle, Capt'n! Someone's took her!'

An exhausted Captain Jack had been sleeping like one dead so it took him a moment or two before he took in what the hysterical Floyd was telling him.

'Who's taken your sister?' he asked, as he sat up on his blanket.

'I don't know,' Floyd cried. 'She went down to the stream to wash herself and when she was late in comin' back I went to see where she was. Her shoes and shirt's there but there ain't any signs of Belle. But I did see the tracks of at least two men, white men, where her clothes were!'

Now fully awake, Captain Jack's face boned over. He could see the picture clearly as if he had seen it happen. He had misread Ketch's reactions twice. The first time, if Garrett hadn't showed up, he would have been killed; now it looked like Belle's life was in danger. And what she could be put through before she was killed sickened him. The bastard Ketch had fooled both him and Slater; he hadn't lit out for Texas but stayed behind to hunt him down.

'Yeah, that sonuvabitch Ketch has taken Belle as hostage. He wants me!' the captain said. 'He and his boys haven't left Artesia, as I was led to believe. It's my fault, I didn't read things right. I reckon I'm gettin' too old for this business.' He gave Floyd a reassuring look. 'Belle will be OK; as I said it's me Ketch wants his dirty hands on for spoilin' his cattle-rustlin' in Lincoln County.'

He didn't tell Floyd that Ketch would also kill him as well as his sister, after Palmer had used her, to make certain there was no one left to finger him as a rustler. But he and Floyd weren't dead yet, a break might come their way, like a damn miracle, he thought. Which was hardly likely, him not being a deeply religious *hombre*.

'Don't worry, Floyd,' he said. 'Ketch will soon let us know he has Belle and wants to parley.'

'How will he do that, Capt'n?' Floyd asked, puzzled.

Captain Jack got to his feet and led Floyd to the mouth of the cave. He stood looking around for a few minutes then pointed to the south-west. 'There, see, Floyd?'

Floyd, gazing along the captain's outstretched arm, saw the column of smoke.

'It's an old Injun way of sendin' a message,' the captain said. 'Ketch's ready to talk, on his terms.'

'I'm goin' with you, Captain Jack,' Floyd said, lips pressed in hard, determined lines. 'It's my sister those no-good sonsuvbitches are holdin'.'

Captain Jack looked Floyd square in the eyes. 'I

wouldn't have expected anything less from you, Floyd,' he said. 'You've turned from a boy into a *hombre* this past week or so. A *bueno hombre* to walk the line with, and that's what we're about to do. I don't know how we can play it when we're eyeballin' the three of them. Ketch will make sure neither of us is carryin' hideaway guns or knives, but I'm tryin' hard to come up with something, believe me, kid.'

Floyd had been doing some quick thinking of his own and thought he had a plan which could give him and the captain a break, albeit only for a few brief seconds or so. Floyd didn't know the time he was hoping to win for them would be long enough to get the upperhand over three hardcase outlaws, and he thought his plan was too wild to tell the captain until he was ready to put it into operation.

Captain Jack buckled on his gunbelt then smiled icily at Floyd. 'Let's go and have that talk with Ketch,' he said. 'We'll not be the only ones who are worryin'. Miss Belle will be doin' more than her share.'

SEVENTEEN

The signal fire had been lit in a clearing in a thick patch of brush and the captain saw that Ketch and Palmer were standing beyond it. The two-gun man was holding one of his fancy-handled pistols at Belle's head, grinning cockily at him and Floyd as they came up to the fire. Out of the corner of his eye, Captain Jack noticed the man he had winged step out of the brush, holding a pistol. At least he knew where the three of them were.

The captain swore under his breath at the sight of Belle's almost naked upper body and frightened mask of a face. Palmer had signed his own death warrant. If it was the last thing he did on this sweet earth, he told himself, he would kill the son-of-a-bitch. He heard Floyd give out an anguished cry and saw his body tense as he made to rush to his sister.

'Stay put!' he said, softly but authoritatively. 'It won't help Belle none seein' Ketch gun you down, will it?'

Reluctantly Floyd listened to reason and held back and the captain breathed more easily. A man aiming to take on three gunmen in a no quarter given or taken shoot-out, had to get himself all set up inside so that he wouldn't think he could be one of the dead when it was all over. The captain's killing lust hadn't reached that peak yet.

Belle gave a low moaning cry on seeing Floyd and the captain walking into the clearing. She had lost her fear of her own blood-chilling fate. Her fears now were all for her brother and Captain Jack. There was no hope of them rescuing her: they were walking to their own deaths. Yet part of her felt proud of them wanting to stand by her side when that terrible moment came.

They stopped just short of the fire, Captain Jack's hand resting lightly on the butt of his sheathed pistol, he and Ketch assessing each other by long, hard-eyed stares.

It was Palmer who spoke first. 'Your sneakin' Injun days are over, old man,' he said, his cock-sureness showing in his voice.

The captain switched his gaze on to him. 'I've come to talk to the bossman, not the hired help,' he said. 'But I'll tell you this, pilgrim, I've come here peaceable, in exchange for the girl. If things don't work out that way then old man or not, I'll put you down for keeps. Even if the back-shootin' asshole behind me kills me first.' He looked back at Ketch. 'M'be I'll get lucky and plug you too, Ketch. Down there along the Rio

Grande I had a rep as a fast gun.'

Palmer's face whitened with mad rage. 'Why you old goat, I'll cut you to pieces!' he yelled, swinging his pistol on to the captain.

'Hold it!' Ketch called out. The old son-of-bitch was giving him the uneasy feeling that he was running the show. He ought to be standing there pleading for the girl's and his own life instead of making threats. Or were they just threats, the blustering talk of a frightened blowhard? His uneasiness grew. He didn't think so. He had seen Indians so full of bullet holes they shouldn't have still been breathing fight back and the old man looked every bit as fierce as a *bronco*. Ketch didn't want to take the chance of ending up dead or badly shot up.

'You for the girl,' he said. 'That's the deal.'

So far so good, the captain thought, they had not been gunned down as soon as they had shown their faces. Though by the glares Palmer was throwing them if he got the job of killing him his dying would be long and painful. Though the longer he could stretch out his terms for the girl's release the more there was of a break coming his and Floyd's way.

'I want the girl and the boy to have the time to get their horses and get to hell outa here, Ketch,' he said. 'Then I'll unbuckle my gunbelt. You can see I ain't carrying a long gun. That's my deal, Ketch, or we can have a small massacre happenin' here.'

The captain had by now worked himself up into accepting a three-to-one gunfight if Ketch turned down his demands. Before Ketch could reply to his ultimatum, Floyd made his move, banking on the captain, as old as he was, of living up to his rep as a man who had out-gunned nine outlaws single-handed. He shot a get-ready glance at the captain, nodding slightly, and saw him raise a quizzical eyebrow which Floyd took to mean he would back his play, though he didn't know what the hell it was.

'Can I give these to my sister?' he said to Ketch, holding up her shirt and shoes. 'She must be feelin' the cold. I ain't armed.'

Ketch gave Floyd a quick, suspicious look before giving a growled, 'OK', then eagle-eyed the old white Indian again.

As a fear-dry-throated Floyd passed the fire, under cover of Belle's shirt he dropped a handful of pistol caps into the centre of the flames. He took two more steps and then the fire blew apart in a series of popping bangs. Then everything happened in a few seconds of flaming guns.

'What the hell!' cried Ketch, jumping back in alarm from the fire, shielding his face with his arms from the flying red-hot embers, and falling right to the ground as Floyd sprang at him, punching and kicking, preventing him from drawing his gun.

The noise brought Belle alive. She flung out one arm wildly, knocking Palmer's gun out of his hand as he was throwing down on Floyd. Captain Jack, fleetingly praising Floyd's action, didn't waste any of the brief time the kid had won for him. His pistol was in his hand with the speed of a born *pistolero*. His first shot hit Palmer in the head, killing him instantly, dropping him to the ground. Then he swung his pistol on to Ketch who had managed to throw off the arms-flailing Floyd and was clawing for his gun while still on the ground.

The captain felt a hot hammer blow on his right leg and infinite pain flashed to every nerve end in his body. Half-bent, fighting off waves of nausea, he kept his hand steady long enough to fire one shot at Ketch before he fell into a deep pit of darkness that mercifully ended his agony. Ketch, his throat torn open by the shell, fell full length on to his back, gasping out his last few dying breaths.

Pike, in a panic at the dramatic and sudden change in his fortunes, came up to Floyd emptying his pistol in a frenzy of wildly-aimed shots. He had wounded the bastard whose fast shooting had swung things against them, now it was the kid's turn to get dead.

Floyd, wincing as Pike's shots kicked up the dust around him, scooped up Ketch's gun and drew a bead on Pike. Then he saw the look of fear on Pike's face, and no more shells came his way. He slow-smiled. The bastard had fired off all his loads. He took his time over the killing. Holding the pistol in both hands he aimed it at Pike as calm and cool as though gunning down a man was

an everyday occurrence to him. Pike was gripping
the gun between his legs trying to reload it with
his one good hand when Floyd's shot hit him high
in the chest, pushing him up on to his toes, his
face creased with pain and the knowing of the
hopelessness of his situation. Floyd's second shot
keeled him over backwards to end up in a crumpled heap on the ground, as dead as the rest of the
Ketch gang. Floyd flung the gun to the ground as
though it had burnt his hand and ran over to
where Captain Jack lay, dreading he and Belle
could be responsible for his death.

Belle, ashen-faced at seeing Palmer's head
burst apart, and some of his blood splashing on to
her bare shoulders, was throwing up. On hearing
Floyd's urgent call of, 'The Capt'n's still alive!' she
wiped her mouth with the back of her hand and
ran across to Floyd, kneeling down beside the
captain.

She shuddered on seeing the shattered bone
and torn bloody tissue that had once been
Captain's Jack's knee and the deathly greyness of
his face.

'Get some blankets, Belle, we've got to keep him
warm!' Floyd spoke sharply, ragged-nerved as the
reaction of his first killing set in. Then, noticing
that his sister was verging on the edge of having
an attack of hysteria, he said, more softly, 'We
can't have the old goat die on us, Belle, can we?
Not when we made him hard-ass all the way from
Presido. You keep the fire built up, I'll ride to the

Jingle Bob for help, OK? To save time I'll mount up on one of those dead asshole's horses.'

Belle reckoned that Floyd was feeling as bad as she was. He had never used strong language in her presence before. In a bolder voice than she was feeling she said, 'I'm OK now. I'll look after the captain. Now you go, Floyd!'

Belle watched him ride away cradling the blanket-wrapped captain in her lap close to a high-flamed fire, listening, tense-faced, to his rasping shallow breathing as he clung on to his life. Her tears this time running freely down her cheeks.

EIGHTEEN

Captain Jack came to gazing at Chisum's face. He grinned wearily at the rancher sitting alongside the bed. 'I've been thinkin' I was in Heaven, then I saw your face and reckoned I musta dreamt it.' The captain's gaze went round the room. 'A fine room you have here, Mr Chisum. How long have I been here?'

'Nigh on three weeks, Capt'n,' replied the rancher, marvelling at the old captain's toughness. He had never expected him to pull through after the operation.

Then the captain asked the question he dreaded the answer to. 'I think I heard the doc say my leg had to come off. Or was that a dream as well?'

Chisum shook his head. 'No, unfortunately that ain't a dream. You'll have to get used to the fact you'll never mount a horse again unaided. Your Ranger days are over.' Chisum gave one of his rare smiles. 'But that don't mean you can't be a sodbuster.'

Captain Jack struggled further up his pillow. 'A sodbuster! Me!' he blurted out. 'Who the hell would be crazy enough to hire a crippled over-the-hill old fart to work his land? Even if I did have a hankerin' to walk behind a plough!'

'Mr Floyd Bishop and Miss Belle would be willing to hire you, and they ain't crazy. They hired you in the first place. If it hadn't been for young Floyd ass-kicking it here, Miss Belle tending to you till we got the doc and the buckboard there you would have been lying buried out back.'

'I ain't accepting any charity, Mr Chisum,' Captain Jack growled. 'And besides, I've upset Billy the Kid. If he breaks outa jail he could come ridin' to the kids' place wantin' to get even with me and Floyd and his sister could get hurt in the crossfire.'

'You've no need to fret what Billy might do, Capt'n,' the rancher replied. 'While you were lying there, keeping us worrying whether or not you were going to live or die, Billy was getting himself shot dead by Marshal Garrett across at Maxwell's ranch. Seemingly – in his infinite wisdom – Governor Wallace granted Billy a full pardon providing he kept on the straight and narrow. But Billy went bad again and now he's no longer riding and shooting his bloody way across the territory. And, furthermore, the kids need you. They ain't mature enough to run the place on their own. Billy, as you rightly know, was not the only bad-ass operating hereabouts.'

Captain Jack, doing some heavy thinking didn't answer him.

Chisum got to his feet. 'I can't sit jawing to you all morning, I've got a spread to run,' he said. 'But think hard about what I've told you. Your Ranger days are over, no matter how much you pine for them.' Chisum stood there for a moment or two, thoughtful-faced, then he smiled again. 'I've a Mex on my payroll who can do wonders with a piece of wood and his knife; he'll make you a new leg in no time at all. After a while you'll be able to move around almost as good as if you had your old leg back.'

Captain Jack had come to a life-changing decision, Chisum was right. There were still wild men prowling around in the territory: home grown West Texans, and agency-jumping Apache. Not a safe place for a young girl to grow up in with only a mere boy to look out for her. While, he knew, he would never plough a straight furrow he was still good with his guns and his rep as a hard-nosed Ranger captain to boot would act as a deterrent to any owl-hooter to give the holding a wide berth. He would be sort of a kind uncle to the kids, something they had never had. That thought gave the captain a good feeling he hadn't had before.

'Mr Chisum!' he called.

Chisum, in the act of closing the door stepped back into the room, looking enquiringly at the captain.

'I would be obliged if you'd tell that Mex you

spoke of to pick himself a nice piece of timber and make me a leg,' Captain Jack said. 'Plantin' time will be soon comin' around and I don't want the kids to think their hired help is a freeloader.'

This time the rancher's grin was a broad-faced smile. 'Me being a cattleman I rate sodbusters one step up from no-good rustlers, but in this case I'll forego a life-long prejudice. I'll have him make that leg for you, *pronto*-like, Captain Jack.'